Tougher than the Rest

MacLarens of Fire Mountain

SHIRLEEN DAVIES

Book One in the MacLarens of Fire Mountain Series

Tougher than the Rest is a work of fiction. Names, characters, places and incidents are either products of the author's imagination or used factiously. Any resemblance to actual events, locales, or persons, living or dead, is wholly coincidental.

ISBN-10: 0989677303
ISBN-13: 978-0-9896773-0-1

Library of Congress Control Number: 2013913877

Cover artwork by idrewdesign.

Description

Niall MacLaren is determined to turn his ranch into the biggest cattle dynasty in the Arizona Territory. The widower will do whatever he must to obtain the political and financial support he needs, even marry a woman he does not love. Nothing will stand in his way.

Katherine is well-bred, educated, and seeks a life away from her cloistered existence in the East. Landing the teaching job in California provides her with the opportunity she seeks. Most importantly, and unlike many of her peers, she will not need a husband to achieve her goals.

When an accident brings them together, mutual desire takes root, threatening to dismantle their carefully laid plans and destroy their dreams. Can either of them afford to be distracted by the passion that unites them—especially when one of them may belong to another?

Dedication

This book is dedicated to my husband, Richard. His unwavering support, endless re-reads, and suggestions, all given in good humor, were a constant encouragement. He is the inspiration for the character, Niall, and I am blessed for the part he plays in my life every day.

Acknowledgements

I want to give a special thank you to Gayle Gross for connecting me with my editor, Regge Episale. Both have unselfishly provided their professional input and suggestions throughout the writing of this book.

Tougher than the Rest

Prologue

Ohio, 1866

Niall covered his ears to drown out the relentless gunfire, but it was no use. The noise continued without pause and echoed throughout the valley surrounding the family's small farm. Their parents had pushed him and his brothers through the trapdoor of a hidden underground room, near the back wall of the barn, and closed it after making them promise not to come out, no matter what they heard. Years of living under the strict rule of their father, Duncan MacLaren, guaranteed they'd do as he demanded.

At last the noise stopped but his ears still rang from the constant bursts of gunfire. The cries of his parents above had ceased long ago. He could no longer hear the whimpering of his seven-year-old twin brothers as they huddled in a far corner. His other brother, Jamie, was with them in the small space, but he made no sound. The chamber smelled stale, locked away from sun and air.

The earthen space was dark, except for small amounts of light passing through slits in the wooden door. He couldn't tell how much time had passed. Niall continued to wait while his heart pounded incessantly. He had to stay calm, and think. Something stirred in the underground chamber. Another minute passed before he sensed, rather than saw, someone try to move past him.

"Stop, Jamie," Niall warned as his brother tried to push him out of the way.

"But Ma and Pa—they're out there," Jamie pleaded, the fear apparent in his trembling voice.

Minutes passed. Unable to wait any longer, Niall shoved at the heavy trapdoor. It was old, the hinges squeaked, but Niall continued to push until he could peer out through the barn to the house beyond. Smoke and debris were everywhere, so much that he could only see vague outlines of clothing, broken chairs, and tools. He looked behind him just as Jamie shoved at his back.

"Let's go, Niall," Jamie hissed.

"No, Jamie." Niall rounded on his younger brother. "You wait here with the twins until I call for you."

Jamie scowled but did as he was told.

Niall climbed out, looking around the barn. His eyes landed on tack ripped from hooks, torn feed sacks, and discarded buckets. Running to the house he found his father, prone, a bullet through his chest, his eyes fixed. Blood soaked the parched ground. Niall wasn't a stranger to death. By the age of fifteen he'd witnessed it several times as a result of the recent war. He knew his father was gone.

A scream formed in his throat as he gazed around to find his mother sprawled half in and half out of the door to their home. The scream, still bottled inside him, escaped as he ran to her. Her head was turned at an odd angle. Her legs twisted within the folds of her long skirt. Niall knelt next to his mother, lifted the lifeless body into his arms, and rocked her. "No!" His mind screamed. But he knew the truth. She was gone. Both of them were gone. He looked up to see the twins, a few feet away, clinging to each other for comfort.

Jamie was standing next to him, gazing down at their mother. His body began to tremble as tears rolled from his eyes. He didn't cry out. Instead, intense rage formed on the young boy's face, and his hands balled into fists as he attempted to quell the hatred burning inside.

Niall looked back down at his mother and pulled her tight against him. Tears streamed down his cheeks, and an odd keening sound emerged as he continued to rock her until no more tears would come and the sky turned dark.

Chapter One

"Darn it, Niall," Jamie said through clenched teeth when they were all settled on the train to St. Louis. At twelve-years-old, he was three years younger than his oldest brother, Niall, but had a short fuse and didn't like to be bossed around.

A month had passed since raiders from West Virginia had crossed into Ohio to pillage the farm and murder their parents. If his father hadn't confided in Niall, just days before, about the money he had saved over many years, they would've been homeless and penniless. After burying their parents, Niall climbed back into the underground room and found two sacks of money. Niall sat stunned. It must have taken their Pa years to save this amount. He knew the bags would have been confiscated along with everything else if the raiders had discovered them.

"What now, Jamie?" Niall asked as he wrapped blankets around the twins and laid his head back against the seat. Although exhausted, scared, and uncertain this was the right decision, he wouldn't give up and change his mind. Pa had said his brother, their Uncle Stuart, who'd immigrated to the United States with him eighteen years earlier, owned a ranch out west, and by God they'd find it. Niall knew his uncle lived in the Arizona Territory near a town called Fire Mountain. He raised cattle. Well, Niall knew farming from working every day under his Pa, and was certain he'd be an asset to his uncle. He'd earn his keep, and that of his brothers, and not allow his uncle to turn them away.

"I don't understand why we can't go to Aunt Margaret's to live. She has a house and servants, food, and lots of room. Why go west when Aunt Margaret is in Charlotte?" Jamie had asked this same question over and over the last couple of weeks. Niall had asked it of himself.

"Because Pa told me we should go to Uncle Stuart's if anything happened," Niall said. He didn't want to tell Jamie their father had called their Aunt Margaret a mean-spirited woman, who never forgave her sister for marrying a Scot. Papa had often said she had a big home, but a small heart. Niall had sent a message to Uncle Stuart before boarding the train, telling him they were heading to Arizona. The oldest MacLaren was determined to get him and his brothers across country. Alive.

"Well, I don't understand, and that's the truth. Papa never said anything to me about going west." Jamie slumped back in to the seat and crossed his arms.

Even though he was barely three years younger than Niall, Pa had never discussed these issues with Jamie, preferring to confide in his oldest son instead. Jamie resented being excluded, and although Niall understood his frustration, he also knew their Pa had thought Jamie too young and temperamental to trust with the information he confided to Niall. Niall thought their Pa had it right. He turned his head to stare out the window as the thickening dark clouds connected to form a solid wall of black. He nodded off as the first spatters of rain signaled the coming storm.

******

St. Louis was large, crowded, noisy, and dirty. Maybe it had some attractive parts, but not from where the boys stood on the crowded walkway. The train master had told Niall they'd need to take a stage the rest of the way to the Arizona Territory. Niall's biggest concern wasn't so much the stage, but the comments the train master made regarding outlaws, Indians, and other dangers. He and Jamie would be fine, but he worried about the twins. How would they do? Well, they'd have to make it work. They had no choice. Niall didn't know how long their money would last, and there was nowhere else to go.

"Hey, kid, look where you're going." The words came from a large, broad-shouldered man who collided with Jamie, sending him sprawling off the depot landing and into the dirt. Jamie jumped up, ran after the man, and pushed him hard from behind. That was Jamie—all action with little forethought regarding consequences—and there were consequences.

"You little hellion," roared the man as he turned to grab Jamie by the collar and throw him into the nearby water trough. The twins gaped as the action unfolded. Niall merely sighed and shook his head before walking up to the stranger to offer his apologies.

"Sorry, mister. He gets a little hotheaded sometimes. We just got to St. Louis and hope to get out of here soon." He glanced back at the three remaining members of his family. "I'll get my brothers and go." Niall didn't want to prolong the fight, and with Jamie, you never knew what to expect. They needed a place to stay, food, baths, and information on how to continue to Arizona.

"Brothers?" The stranger hadn't seen the twins a few feet away.

"Yeah, my brothers and I are headed for the Arizona Territory. Our uncle has a ranch there." The idea of supplying too much information to a stranger didn't sit well with Niall.

"The four of you are traveling, by yourselves, all the way to Arizona, and no adult?" The stranger glanced around at the circle of boys, surprised the four of them were traveling alone. The oldest was tall, but still didn't appear to be older than thirteen, maybe fourteen.

"Hell, mister, I'm fifteen and my brother is twelve. We've done fine so far, and we'll do fine the rest of the way." Defiance laced his voice.

"Fifteen, huh? Well, that is right old. You know how to protect them? Use a gun?"

"Of course I can use a gun. Our Pa taught us how to shoot, and we had to hunt much of our food." He regarded his brothers, worried about the same things the stranger mentioned, but there was no one else to do this, just him.

"I mean a pistol. You know how to use one of these?" The stranger pulled out a magnificent Colt revolver. "You ever shot a gun like this?"

Niall's eyes widened as he stared at the gun. He'd seen lots of pistols but never a gun as beautiful as this one. Sleek, shiny, with an ivory handle. How would it feel to hold such a gun? Hell, what would the gun feel like to shoot? Ma didn't like pistols. Said they were meant for a single purpose. Killing people. She held with rifles for shooting game and basic protection, but a pistol? No. A pistol was for another use altogether.

Ma. The thought of her brought pain to his heart. If he were older, without the responsibility of his brothers, he would've gone after the murderers and killed every one of them.

"Uh, no, sir, never shot one of those. I never had the chance." Niall felt insecure. Maybe he wasn't as prepared for the trip as he thought.

"My name is Garner, Trent Garner. Where you boys staying?"

Niall studied Garner for a minute. Maybe it wouldn't hurt to know someone familiar with the town. "I'm Niall. Niall MacLaren. This is Jamie and the twins are Will and Drew. We don't have a place yet. We were on our way to find a room when Jamie collided with you."

MacLaren? He knew a MacLaren in the Arizona Territory. Fire Mountain area. Coincidence? Garner didn't believe in coincidences, but he wouldn't press Niall. The boy had enough on his mind.

"Hey, he collided with me." Jamie protested.

Garner ignored the outburst. "Well, tell you what. I'll take you to the hotel where I stay. Find out if a room's available. Grab your stuff and let's go." Garner didn't wait for an answer. He left them standing and started walking at a brisk pace down the road.

******

"Afternoon, Marshal," the desk clerk glanced up from his paperwork as the small group walked into the hotel lobby.

Marshal? Why didn't Garner say he was a marshal? Niall wondered.

"Got me some friends here who need a room. What do you have?"

"One room, baths for all, three bits per night. Food is extra." No way the clerk would let those four boys, in their dirty condition, sleep in his beds, even if they were friends of the marshal.

"Done." Garner tossed coins to the clerk for one night, got the key, and started up the stairs. "Hey, you boys coming or not?"

That shook Niall out of his trance. He and the brothers scrambled up the stairs behind the marshal.

"You hear that, Niall? The guy's a marshal. Why didn't he say that right off?" Jamie whispered as he followed his brother down the hall to their room.

"Yeah, I heard. Guess he has his reasons," Niall said as Garner opened the door to their room.

The room was small but clean, with places all four could bed down. It looked over the main street and dust blew through the sheer curtains when Niall opened the window to peer out. Shutting the window, he turned to survey the room. There sure was a lot of furniture in the small space. An oak bureau sat against one wall with a pitcher of water and basin sitting off-center, an oil lamp to the side, and a mirror at the back. Another large piece of furniture rested along a second wall. When opened,

15

he saw a bar for clothes. He recalled his Ma used to call these wardrobes, hinting more than once how much she would have liked to own one. Again, his gut twisted, and he wondered once more when this gnawing sensation would end.

"Clean up boys and I'll meet you downstairs in an hour," the marshal said as he closed to the door.

An hour later they met Garner in the hotel dining room. Niall couldn't remember ever being in a place this grand. Garner ordered the special all around, and watched the boys devour their food, almost licking their plates clean. Garner had never seen four young boys eat as these did. Must've been awhile since they'd enjoyed a full meal. *Tough bunch of kids*, he thought as he nursed his second cup of coffee. What were four boys doing traveling to the Arizona Territory? What about their folks? They were no more prepared for the trip than most easterners he met.

"Where you from?" Garner looked to Niall as the boys dug into their dessert.

"Ohio," Niall said between bites. He didn't want to talk about Ohio, his parents and their murder, or the boys' future.

"And your folks?"

Niall set down his fork, tried to straighten in his seat, but his shoulders drooped under the weight of the responsibilities that had passed to him.

"Murdered," he finally said. "Raiders came across the border. Murdered them, stole everything we had, and burned what was left." He paused to take a sip of the sarsaparilla Garner had ordered for each. "Pa said we should go to our uncle's ranch if

16

anything ever happened. So that's where we're headed, and we'll make it, too." Niall stiffened his spine and looked straight into the marshal's eyes.

Garner considered the boy's words, resigning himself to their situation. "Well then, tomorrow let's do what we can to help you get to Arizona alive."

******

They met the marshal in the dining room again the next morning. Garner told them what to expect the rest of their trip including rough terrain, endless dust, bad food, and unknown dangers. "It's the unknown dangers that'll kill you," he said before leading them to an open area back behind the hotel, where he addressed all four of them.

"I'm going to show Niall and Jamie how to inspect, load, and shoot this gun. I don't want you two," pointing to Drew and Will, "to stand any closer to us than right there." He indicated a place about eight feet back, next to a rock. "Do you understand me?" The twins signaled their understanding by running the eight feet as ordered.

"Boys, this gun is for protection. Not for fun, not to pick fights, and not to show off, but to defend yourself if you get in a bad situation. Got that so far?" Niall and Jamie nodded their understanding.

Garner proceeded to spend the next three hours educating the boys about handling a gun. He repeated every instruction several times until the boys got it right. Niall was good, very good. But Jamie took to it as if he was born with a gun in his hand. It was instinctive. Garner had witnessed this uncanny aptitude before, and the insight didn't

17

thrill him. The boy would have to sort out his skill, and what to do with it, as he got older.

They went through the entire process again after dinner. By suppertime, the marshal decided they'd progressed enough to take them to the gunsmith and negotiate a sale. Garner introduced the boys and explained what they needed. The gunsmith responded with an older, but clean, Colt revolver, and a couple boxes of shells. Within minutes Niall owned his first gun.

******

The following morning Garner helped the boys load their gear and climb into the stage headed for Fort Smith.

"You boys stay together and remember what I told you."

Jamie, Drew, and Will nodded at the marshal, but Niall lifted his hand to shake that of the one person who'd gone out of his way to help them. Educate them.

"Thanks, Marshal Garner, for everything. We won't forget you." Niall's voice broke as gratitude filled him. In just two days Niall had formed a bond with the man. He'd miss him.

The marshal nodded, shaking the young man's hand firmly before letting go. Then, in an instant, the driver smacked the reins, and they were gone.

Unease plagued Garner at sending them off alone, but he'd done what he could. He'd taught them how to use the Colt, and talked the gunsmith into accepting almost nothing for the gun. The four MacLaren brothers had made it this far. He had to believe the rest of their journey would be safe, but the odds were against them. Nevertheless, Garner went back to the telegraph office to send a message to an old friend.

Chapter Two

Niall jumped off the stage in Antelope Springs. He surveyed their surroundings, searching for anyone who might be looking for four boys. It had been a long, dusty, uneventful trip, which was good and bad. Both Niall and Jamie had hoped to run into a little more action after Garner had taught them how to handle the pistol, but nothing. No Indians, no stage robbers. Just a broken down wagon abandoned along the side of the trail, and a few skeletons—cattle probably.

"What now, Niall?" A small hand grabbed his and tugged before letting go.

"Don't know, Drew, except we're all hungry. So the first thing is to get some food." Niall smiled down at his two youngest brothers. Jamie had stayed by the stage to catch the two bags thrown to him by the driver. Not much, but at least they had some clothes, a small picture of their parents, and his Ma's bible. They'd used one bag of money. The other remained full, and Niall realized it would have to last long enough for them to find their uncle.

Niall turned in a circle again, but the fact was there wasn't much to the small town. Antelope Springs was a tiny stop on the road with what appeared to be a small trading post, livery, and saloon. Maybe their uncle never received the telegrams. Maybe he just didn't want them at his ranch.

"You wouldn't be Niall MacLaren, would you?" The stranger approached from the livery and headed straight for Niall.

"Who's asking?" Jamie spoke up before Niall could respond.

"Got word from Marshal Trent Garner that four boys were traveling in this direction, possibly looking for Stuart MacLaren. Is that you?"

"You're a friend of Marshal Garner?" Niall was stunned. He couldn't believe the marshal hadn't mentioned he might know their uncle.

The marshal's an old friend of your uncle's. The name MacLaren clicked with him and he thought you might be Stuart's kin. Your uncle sent me to fetch the four of you. His ranch is to the south. I'm here to take you, if that's still what you want."

"You know the marshal, too?" Jamie looked up at the man sent to help them.

"Met him a time or two, but it's your uncle who knows him. Going on ten years, I believe. And, of course, Gus, over there by the wagon." The man pointed to a tall, wiry cowboy standing next to a couple of horses harnessed to a supply wagon. "He and Garner met just before Gus left the U.S. Marshals Service to work for your uncle. Garner passes through Fire Mountain sometimes on business. He always stops at the ranch to visit with Gus, your aunt, and your uncle. Good man."

The stranger extended his hand. "Pete Cantlin, and I assume you're Niall."

Niall shook the man's hand and nodded.

"I needed to pick up a few horses your uncle bought from a rancher in Antelope Springs anyway, so your timing turned out perfect. I could use your help if you can ride. If not, the supply wagon has plenty of room for the four of you. Meet me at the livery in an hour." He turned and walked away without a backward glance.

******

Cantlin had been glad to see that the two oldest boys were experienced riders. He'd brought a couple of extra horses and gear, hoping the boys would be able to help him take the small herd south. He'd been surprised at how well they'd caught on. Niall selected the paint and Jamie the bay, and each had taken full responsibility for his horse.

Two days later the boys stood on a hill overlooking a green valley with hundreds of cattle being driven by at least a dozen horsemen. Real cowboys. The boys had seen them before, but none made a more lasting impression than those on their uncle's land, whooping and yelling to each other while moving their horses with ease to guide the errant strays back into the main herd.

"Beautiful, isn't it?" Cantlin came up behind them on his horse and leaned over the saddle horn as he surveyed the scene below.

"Are we there, Niall?" Will jumped up and down, pointing to the valley below.

"Is this Uncle Stuart's?" Drew, the shyest of the four, asked. His question underscored how ready he was to finish the journey.

"This is it boys. Your uncle is the one at the far right, riding the big roan."

All heads swiveled and the four stared at the man they'd traveled so far to meet—the man who would determine their future—the man who might turn them away.

"Let's go." Cantlin turned his horse toward the valley floor and motioned the boys to follow.

******

Stuart took off his hat and gazed up the hill as some riders and a wagon started to descend. The sun was sinking behind him, but he had no trouble making out two small figures riding with Gus in the wagon, and two larger figures riding alongside Pete. Cantlin stood out with his tall figure sitting straight on the black gelding. *So the man did it*, Stuart thought. *He found my nephews.*

What the hell would he do with them? Fifteen years had passed since he'd seen the oldest, Niall. Stuart had left for the frontier just after Niall's birth. Duncan and Elizabeth's house just couldn't handle the growing family and him. Duncan had begged his brother to stay, saying he'd enlarge the house. Stuart was adamant. Farming was Duncan's dream, not his. The west and cattle ranching drew him. He left for his new life a few days later.

And what a life it had become. Stuart met an older rancher, without heirs, who taught him ranching in return for taking care of the man during a long illness. Some might say it was luck, others that he'd tricked the old man, but he knew the truth. Working the ranch during the day and tending to Ike through his long illness had taken a tremendous toll on Stuart. He'd handled the hiring, firing,

23

buying, and selling, as well as the occasional raids by Apaches. Ike had believed in him, taught him the business, and, in the end, rewarded Stuart with the land. He'd grown the operation to at least twice its original size. His pride in the ranch was evident to anyone who met him.

His one regret was not having boys of his own. Alicia was the love of his life, but after several years of trying, they both accepted the fact she'd never be able to have a child. Alicia believed the boys coming to their ranch to be a true gift from God. Stuart wasn't so sure.

******

"Pete." Stuart called out as the group got within twenty feet.

"Boss," Cantlin said and nodded toward his companions. The appearance of the four boys and expressions on their faces told it all. Wonder, fear, hope—all exposed in varying degrees as they stared at their uncle.

So this man is our uncle, thought Niall as he inspected the man atop the large horse. Curly, reddish-brown hair, the color of red clay, peeked out from under his hat. His skin was coarse from long hours in the sun, but he sat ramrod straight, and stared at them with eyes the color of green moss. The same eyes as their Pa.

Niall rode forward.

"Uncle Stuart, I'm Niall, your nephew. Mr. Cantlin said you received the message from the marshal and are expecting us."

"That's so, Niall. Also got the first telegram, the one sent before you left for St. Louis. Duncan always knew to send you here if anything happened. Sorry it came to this, but..." The childless rancher felt a lump in his throat. He had no idea how to respond to these boys even though he'd spent years owning a ranch populated by up to fifteen men between the ages of sixteen and sixty. Stuart cleared his throat. "Pete, take my place and finish up here. Gus and I will take the boys to meet their aunt."

"Sounds good, Boss," Pete said and took off toward the other wranglers.

Stuart turned his horse south, leaving the boys with no choice but to follow him to their new home and an uncertain future.

******

The last part of their journey was short, perhaps a couple of miles at most, but Niall wasn't thinking about the distance. His mind tried to sort out the response from their uncle. Were they welcome or an extra burden? What would their aunt think of them? Niall realized he had little time to worry the issue when he saw the big house appear around a bend.

"Alicia. Come out and meet your nephews," Uncle Stuart yelled while dismounting to climb the porch steps. "Niall, you and the other boys come on in to meet your Aunt Alicia. I know she's anxious to see you."

"Yes, sir." Niall motioned for his brothers to get moving.

"Niall, what do you think?" Jamie had walked up beside his older brother.

25

"I think we better get in the house quick," Niall said while taking in the large two-story house. "Come on, Drew, Will. Let's go." He watched as the twins scrambled from the wagon and ran to his side. As a group, they walked up the steps and followed their uncle into the house.

"Well, you must be Niall." A short, slender woman with brown hair tied into a tight bun walked up and pulled him into a hug before he had a chance to respond. She stepped back and smiled at him. "I'm your Aunt Alicia, and we are so glad all of you are here. Now, introduce me to my other nephews."

In turn, Jamie, Drew, and Will received the same warm smile and hug. They felt intense relief by the welcome, and began to relax as they took in the spacious room.

"Is this our home now, Aunt Alicia?" Will walked up to his aunt with a huge smile on his face.

"Why, yes, Will, this is your home, for as long as you want it to be." The knot she'd carried in her stomach all day began to lessen. She hadn't realized until this moment how much she needed her nephews to like their new home. "For as long as all of you want it to be, this is your home," she said again so all the boys understood.

"I imagine the four of you must be hungry. Let's get some food in you, then we'll show you around." Aunt Alicia ushered her nephews into the large dining room where Uncle Stuart already sat at the head of the table.

"Thought you boys had decided to leave," their uncle said in a gruff tone as the boys took their places at the table. The room went silent. Their

26

uncle stared from one to another, his eyes settling on Niall. *Damn, but he looks like his father did at that age*, Stuart thought, but he pushed it aside. "Well, dig in. The food's not going to jump on your plate by itself." And with that, their new life at the MacLaren ranch in Fire Mountain began to unfold.

Chapter Three

Philadelphia 1878
12 years later

"Father, I'll be fine. I know it's a long trip, and you're concerned, but I need to do this. Alone." Kate loved her father. They had become very close since her mother had passed away several years before. Other than his work, she was his life, and he tended to direct it the way he directed his job.

"Katherine, I will repeat myself. You're not traveling to California alone. If I can't go with you, we will find a suitable companion. You have never been farther west than Texas, and the territories are still wild. It's not the place for a young lady to be traveling alone." From his perspective, this discussion had ended and wasn't negotiable.

"Father, I grew up in Texas. Well, at least until I started finishing school. I understand better than most women what to expect." Katherine sighed. This topic had been discussed many times. She knew her father understood her capabilities, but somehow his confidence in her never figured into their discussions about the future. "I've sent the school board my acceptance and need to be in California in two months to setup the schoolroom and order materials. How will I find a companion who can be ready to travel on short notice, not to mention someone you'll accept?" Frustration surged through Kate, but in her heart, she accepted her father was doing what he thought best. Even though she considered herself a confident, self-assured adult, he saw her as his daughter and his responsibility.

"I won't discuss this issue further, Kate. Find a companion with acceptable references I can check. Only then can you go, and not before." Her father walked to the door before turning.

"Katherine, you know I'm proud of you and what you've accomplished. My love couldn't be stronger. But since I cannot accompany you, I need you to do this my way so your journey has the best chance of ending well. Do this for me."

Kate had worked hard to obtain a teaching credential from the Normal School. She'd found a position in Philadelphia right away and had already taught a couple of years. Even though she'd spent the first part of her life in Texas, her father had expected her to continue to teach and live in the East. She found her desire to explore the other half of the country too strong. With the encouragement of the administrators at the Normal School, she'd applied several months ago for a new position in Los Angeles, a fast growing city in California. Weeks had gone by without any word, so Kate assumed the position had been filled. To her surprise and delight, an urgent message had arrived a week ago stating she'd been hired, and her traveling expenses would be repaid upon her arrival. It was early June. School started in late August. Not much time.

******

"Aunt Alicia!" Will searched for his aunt in the barn, but no luck. All right, where else could she be?

Not in the house, in her garden, or in the barn. Of course—up the hill at the small family plot.

Will's shouts penetrated Alicia's thoughts. She rose to turn toward the house and her nephew. Will was already pounding up the hill to meet her. Each Sunday, Alicia spent time at Stuart's grave, still trying to reconcile herself to her loss. The most important person in her life was no longer by her side. A freak accident during a cattle drive five years ago had taken him from her and the boys.

But they were no longer boys. The twins, at nineteen, appeared alike, but the similarity ended on the outside. Both had dark, russet-brown hair, much like their uncle's, that shone dark gold in the sun. Both stood tall at over six feet each, and possessed strong bodies and broad shoulders. Few people could tell them apart until they spoke.

Tireless and outspoken, Will loved the ranch to distraction. If he ever left it would be over someone's dead body. Drew possessed a quiet nature. The peacemaker of the family, he loved to solve problems, and yearned for an education, which would take him away in little more than a year. Both could ride most men to ground, both understood the cattle business as well as their older brothers did, and both were smitten with the same girl.

"The Jacobsons are heading over the rise and should be here soon. Need any help?" Will looked hopeful as Alicia tried to hide her smile. Will never volunteered to help in the house. Other than helping with meal cleanup and repairs, none of the boys volunteered unless she was gravely ill, which meant bedridden.

"No, but thank you, Will. I have everything ready. Would you alert Drew while I check the food?"

"Well," Will hedged, "I thought I'd welcome them first, and find the others once the Jacobsons are settled in the house. Maybe I'll take Mr. Jacobson out to visit the new mare."

Will was so transparent. He wanted first crack at talking to Emily Jacobson. At seventeen, Emily possessed a striking appearance with long, flowing, brown hair and soft, blue eyes. She came from a hard-working neighboring ranch family who'd welcomed the boys when they had arrived years ago. Alicia understood why both were smitten. Emily had a natural ability to put people at ease and a contagious laugh. Drew and Will hadn't been too discreet in their competition for Emily's attentions for years. To her credit, Emily had treated both equally, with no hint of which one she might favor, if either. But if Alicia had to bet, she'd pick Will as Emily's eventual choice.

"Sure, Will. Just tell the others soon so they can clean up." Alicia moved past him to the back door and stepped into their sprawling ranch house.

******

"Wonderful supper, Alicia. We always enjoy coming out here to visit." John Jacobson had been Stuart's closest friend and missed him almost as much as Alicia did. His wife, Marie Ellen, was close to Alicia. Unlike Alicia, who'd been a true partner on the ranch with her husband, Marie Ellen possessed a more reserved personality, preferring to run the house and entertain. The MacLaren and Jacobson ranches were the two most prosperous in the region.

"Aunt Alicia, we're back!" A short fireball burst into the dining room.

"Beth, what have you been told about running in the house and yelling?" Alicia scolded. At six, Beth still had a lot to learn. Without a mother, it fell to her aunt to instruct.

"Hello, everyone," Niall called as he strolled into the house and extended his hand to John. Niall always enjoyed Sunday dinners with the Jacobsons, but he had another matter requiring his attention every week on that particular day.

"Niall, sorry you weren't able to join us for supper." John took Niall's hand and shook it warmly. At five feet eleven inches, John stood a few inches shorter than Niall, with graying hair, a slim frame, and firm handshake. Strong as ever, he was a force in the area, the same as Stuart had been before his death.

"Yes, well, I've been having Sunday dinner in town the last few weeks," Niall replied.

"It's really boring, and the food isn't as good as Aunt Alicia's, and Mrs. van Deelin stares at Pa, and asks me to go outside to play," Beth pouted. She jumped into Will's arms and he twirled her around.

"Mrs. van Deelin?" Marie Ellen asked, casting a sideways glance at Alicia.

Alicia just shrugged while continuing to clear the table. His aunt felt the time had come for Niall to move on, but Jocelyn van Deelin? Somehow it didn't fit.

Niall hadn't courted a respectable woman since his wife, Camille, had died six years earlier giving birth to Elizabeth, or Beth, as she preferred to be called. He didn't hide the fact he frequented the Desert Dove, spending time with Gloria, the owner of the saloon and a long-time friend, but he had never shown any interest in a replacement for his beloved Camille.

Niall cleared his throat, nodded at Marie Ellen, and headed toward the kitchen. A piece of pie and coffee sounded good. Hell, even water sounded good if it would save him from questions about Jocelyn.

He knew Jocelyn had alienated many of the townspeople after her husband had died a year ago. A wealthy industrialist from the east, Walter had become a town leader. He'd worked tirelessly to keep Fire Mountain in the forefront of Arizona politics. After his death, Jocelyn put a quick end to all of his work with the clear intention of selling most of the van Deelin interests to move back to New York. Her intentions didn't matter to Niall. He had but one reason for courting Widow van Deelin, a reason he wasn't yet prepared to share with his family.

"Come on, squirt," Will called to Beth, "let's go check on the new foal of yours. Emily, would you like to join us?" Will grabbed his hat and opened the front door. John, Emily's father, pushed out of his chair to follow them outside. "I think I'll join you and let the ladies ponder Niall's future." Niall's business wasn't his concern, but John just didn't understand how Jocelyn van Deelin fit with the boy he knew.

Chapter Four

The trip was miserable. Hot, dusty, long, with poor food and foul accommodations. Kate kept a positive disposition through it all. Her companion, Mrs. Stelford, did not.

Fifteen years older than Kate, Mrs. Stelford seemed three times that in actions and appearance. Widowed several years before, she'd lived with her spinster-sister in Philadelphia, providing music lessons to young socialites, and living through her books. She'd traveled extensively in her youth and had been exuberant about the trip during her interview with Kate's father. There was no sign of exuberance now.

Kate hoped she'd be able to endure the woman's disapprovals the rest of the trip. Mrs. Stelford's complaints seemed to persist unabated, as did her constant banter about their fellow passengers. No one met her expectations, and none should be trusted, she had confided to Kate several times. But, Kate reminded herself, she had been willing to travel to California with less than two weeks notice. The woman had a married sister in San Francisco who had assured Mrs. Stelford her music skills would be well regarded in a town begging for cultured residents. Perhaps Kate would get a break when they reached Phoenix.

The town of Phoenix surprised Kate. It seemed new compared to most settlements along their route, and appeared to be growing. Travelers frequented the town when making their way to

California. Kate and Mrs. Stelford would stay at least one night before finalizing their journey to Los Angeles.

"Papa, wait for me. You're walking too fast!" Kate heard the child moments before being knocked to the ground by a tall, broad-shouldered man who'd turned to find the child.

"Ah hell, I mean, I'm sorry, ma'am. Are you okay? Let me help you up."

"Katherine, are you all right?" Mrs. Stelford had missed being included in the collision, but stood with her hands on her hips and stared wild-eyed at the offending man. "As for you," she directed her anger his way, "you need to pay attention, and...." The rest faded away as the man bent to offer his hand to his female victim and mumble additional words of apology.

Kate glanced up to grasp his hand, and looked into the most striking green eyes she'd ever seen. *Emerald green¬*, she thought, the color of her mother's favorite dress. Emerald eyes that twinkled with slight amusement as he peered down at her. The effect was immediate and disconcerting. She couldn't ever remember meeting a more handsome man.

"Ma'am?" The stranger prompted when Kate didn't respond.

"Yes, I'm fine," she stammered as he drew her to a standing position in front of him. Kate attempted to adjust her clothing and brush off the dust. "I was staring at the buildings, trying to figure out where to go next, and wasn't watching." She jabbered on, making no real sense while at the same time trying to get a better view of the man without him knowing.

He stood well over six feet, with broad shoulders, and hair the color of midnight peeking out from under his lowered hat. He wore a blue chambray shirt with tan vest and pants. His belt appeared to be hand-tooled, and fastened with a magnificent silver buckle. Kate's gaze moved up to his face, and into the most incredible smile she'd ever seen.

"Are you sure you're all right, ma'am?" He chuckled softly. "I don't believe I've ever had a lady look me over the way you've been doing the last couple of minutes." He leaned in close as he said those last words, watching Kate's face redden before his eyes.

Kate jumped back, ran a hand through her hair in an attempt to compose herself, and leaned down to pick up her satchel and reticule. Now she just wanted the stranger to walk on and not draw any more attention to them. She was fine, but she wouldn't be if Mrs. Stelford kept making a fuss and the man kept standing there staring at her.

She drew herself up to her full height of five feet four inches and glared straight into those magnificent eyes. "Perhaps you could direct us to a hotel?" Kate asked in a dismissive tone as she twisted the gold band on her left hand. Her father had given Kate her mother's wedding band as she boarded the train. For safekeeping, he'd said. Kate knew the truth. He'd passed something important on to his daughter. She'd gotten into the habit of staring at the ring when she was bored, or twisting the band when she felt stressed. Something about the way this man stared at her made her want to twist it off and hide it in her reticule.

"Well, we don't get here too often, but Farrell's boarding house is down the street." He gestured, indicating the direction. "They might take you in for a few days. The Grant Hotel is the other way. It's a little expensive but clean, and you'll have good food. The only other place I know to stay is in one of the upstairs rooms at Red's Palace. Probably not the best place." The man smiled, grabbed the hand of the young girl who'd been hiding behind him, and turned to walk off.

"No, probably not," Kate said to his back, her heart still thudding in her chest. *Strange man,* she thought as she and her companion made their way to the Grant Hotel.

******

"Well, there you two are." Alicia stood outside the mercantile where they shopped a couple of times a year when Niall traveled to Phoenix for business.

"Papa walked too fast for me, and he knocked a lady down, and another lady yelled at him," Beth blurted out as she ran up to her aunt.

"Niall?" Alicia turned a questioning look at Niall.

"It was nothing. Sorry to hold you up. Where to now?" Niall wanted to end their business and move on. His heart still pounded from the encounter with one of the loveliest women he'd ever laid eyes on. Silky blonde hair that shone in the bright sun, sparkling blue eyes, and translucent skin, resembling alabaster, which had turned a deep red when she was caught staring at him. She was slight of stature. He guessed maybe five four or five five. It was a wonder he hadn't crushed her when they collided. But it was her beautifully curved, soft lips, almost raspberry in color, he couldn't stop thinking about. Niall did like raspberries.

"We should finish up and start for the Carlson ranch before it gets any later," he said, more to move his thoughts away from the attractive stranger and back into safer territory. They'd start the journey back to Fire Mountain tomorrow, but not before spending the night at one of the best horse ranches in the territory.

"I'm finished, and the wagon is loaded, so I believe we're ready to visit Rand and Julia." Alicia had known the Carlson's for many years and seized any excuse to visit.

By wagon, it was quite a distance to the beautiful ranch house Rand had built almost thirty years before. The Carlson Rim Ranch was north of Phoenix. Alicia and Niall always enjoyed stopping to enjoy the warm reception the Carlsons provided.

Rand had been one of his uncle's closest friends and had become almost another father figure to Niall after his uncle had died. Rand and his wife Julia had spent a month at the MacLaren's after Stuart's death, helping Niall and the brothers with ranch business, while Julia helped Alicia, who'd taken the death hard. The families had stayed close even though distance kept them from being together more than a couple of times a year.

Chapter Five

The next morning found the MacLarens on the trail early. The wagon slowed them down, but Alicia drove better than most men, and Beth's constant chatter made the miles go by fast. Niall rode ahead on Zeus most of the time while keeping an eye out for danger. No attacks on travelers had been reported in quite a while, but this desolate country had few ranches and only two towns.

"Papa, look!" Beth screamed at her father, who'd ridden ahead of the wagon. They were outside of Watsonville and would be home in a few more hours.

Niall turned as his daughter pointed to the stage bearing down on them.

The day was windy, dry, and dusty, and as the stage approached, Niall knew something wasn't quite right. The horses ran much too fast and appeared to be out of control.

"Aunt Alicia, get off the trail. Now!" Niall drew closer to help guide their team off the dirt road into a flat area that would be safe from the out-of-control stage.

Alicia glanced over her shoulder while pulling the wagon off the road to avoid a collision. That's when Niall spotted the driver slumped over, with the reins slack in his hands. Screams could be heard coming from inside the coach. Niall responded without thinking, nudging Zeus and charging towards the retreating stage.

Zeus was fast, but as Niall approached the stage's back wheels, the horses veered to the right to avoid a large boulder. The stage careened over a small embankment with the front wheels hitting a patch of rock, sending the coach rolling down the hill onto its side before coming to rest against a stand of large cactus.

Zeus had barely stopped when Niall jumped off and ran to the crumpled mess, his boots crunching on the sand and gravel. He unhitched the horses, jumped onto the side of the coach to peer inside, but he saw no movement, just several sets of tangled legs and arms. From where he stood, it appeared there might be four passengers. A soft moan emerged from someone and a muted curse from another.

"Let me help you," Niall offered to no one in particular. He slid into the coach when another moan came from one of the women.

"It's all right. Help is here." In an instant Niall recognized the older woman who'd yelled at him as well as the younger woman he'd run over on the walkway in Phoenix.

Just my luck, Niall thought as he squatted down to examine the older woman whose neck was bent at an odd angle. He checked her pulse. Nothing. He pivoted over to the younger woman who continued to moan but hadn't moved. Two other passengers, both men, tried to stand. They cursed as each attempted to untangle themselves from the two women. One held an arm that appeared broken, and the other favored a mangled leg.

"Beth, you stay in the wagon. Niall, what can I do?" Alicia yelled from outside the coach.

"Can either of you climb out to help me with the women?" Niall directed his question to the men, who hadn't shown much progress in standing without falling back down.

"I seem to have only one good arm, but I think I can get out okay." He was around twenty, possibly part Indian, somebody accustomed to being outside. "I'd rather stay if I can help you with the other passengers," the young man said.

"Nope, but thanks. Best thing you can do is get out of the coach so I have room to check on the others." Niall's eyes never left the beautiful, injured woman who still lay motionless.

"Aunt Alicia, one of the passengers is going to try to climb out. He has a bad arm and will need some help."

"Send him on out," Alicia called back. Somehow the young man slid out the opening and sat down by one of the larger boulders while Alicia tended to him.

"Don't know if I can get out with this leg, but I'll try." The other man gritted his teeth while holding a leg that wouldn't support his weight. He was older than the other male, closer to thirty, a little shorter, and it didn't appear he did much physical work. "But first, I need to check the women. I'm a doctor. I might need some help finding my supplies in the ruins. They're in a small trunk, black with brass fittings." Beads of sweat formed on the man's face and Niall hoped the man held it together long enough to help the other passengers.

"I heard him," Alicia shouted, already starting to search for the supply trunk. One of the trunks had opened upon hitting the ground, sending dresses, personal belongings, and papers in all directions. While Alicia searched, she listened as Niall told the doctor about the older woman. The doctor found no pulse, nodded his agreement, and moved to the younger woman who still hadn't gained consciousness.

"We'll need to get her outside. I don't find any breaks, but won't know for certain until we get her out of here. You ready?" The doctor's gaze lifted to Niall, who nodded.

Between all of them, they lifted the young woman out. Although the doctor confirmed no broken bones, she still hadn't woken up. Her soft moans filled the air.

"We need to get her to a town. First, I'll set this one's arm," the doctor motioned to the other man, who had introduced himself as Sam Browning, "and try to set my leg. It's not broken, maybe a bad sprain. I'll need your help with both."

The doctor seemed to be holding it together. Niall was of half a mind not to let the man leave once they arrived in Fire Mountain. Fire Mountain needed another doctor with their long-term doc moving up in years. This one seemed promising.

An hour later Alicia, Beth, and Sam sat on the small bench of the wagon. The doctor rested in the back with the younger woman and the bodies of her companion and the stagecoach driver. They needed to head straight for Fire Mountain. Neither

Watsonville nor the small settlement of Shelton had much in the way of medical help.

The trip took longer than expected due to their slow pace. The sky was dark when the wagon pulled up to a decent sized building. The structure served as the local clinic as well as the home of the town's doctor.

Niall wasted no time getting Doc Minton out of bed to open the clinic. He laid the woman on a table and stood, staring at her. She seemed so young with her eyes closed and her face at rest. Her shiny blonde hair was now disheveled, and her clothes torn, but he still thought her beautiful. He guessed her to be seventeen or eighteen. It was hard to tell, but either way she was much too young for him. Niall shook his head at the direction of his thoughts and glanced up at Doc Minton.

"Who is she?" The doctor started moving his hands over her body to check for broken bones.

"I don't know. She hasn't woken up since the stage accident. She must have hit her head," Niall responded.

A voice from the doorway carried into the room. "Couldn't find any broken bones when we checked, but..." the voice trailed off.

Niall saw the other doctor trying to make his way into the small exam room.

"Doc Minton, this is Doctor McCauley, another passenger. Hurt his leg. We setup a splint, but you might want to check him out." Niall returned his gaze to the woman. *Why doesn't she wake up?* He never knew of a time when someone didn't wake up after a few minutes. This had been hours.

45

"Doctor Minton, please call me Caleb." The younger man offered his hand in greeting.

"Pleased to meet you, Caleb. So she hasn't woken at all since the accident?" Doc Minton asked the other doctor.

Another soft moan escaped her lips, her head moved to the left, and she tried to open her eyes. First one eye and then the other.

"Oh, the lights, please¬¬––they're so bright." Her words were whispered. She tried to raise her arm to cover her eyes.

"Let me adjust these lights so I can take a better look at you, young lady." Doc Minton was somewhere in his seventies. About no one could remember a time when he didn't practice in Fire Mountain. He had worked as the doctor at Fort Winston and then moved into town with his wife and two sons. His wife had passed a few years ago, but his two sons still lived in the area, one a lawyer who represented many of the local ranchers, and one who owned a ranch on the other side of the valley from the MacLaren spread.

"So, what's your name, young lady?" The doctor continued his examination as he waited for her response.

"I'm....my name is....Um, I'm...." she stammered and tried to focus. Confusion and slight panic crossed her face as her eyes came to rest on Doc Minton.

"Kate. I believe you introduced yourself as Katherine, but preferred Kate, when you boarded the stagecoach." Caleb tried to recall a last name, but nothing came. She remained silent, but her eyes blinked as she gazed from one man to another, trying to reconcile what Caleb said with her own confused thoughts. She came up with nothing.

After a few more minutes of speaking with Kate, the doctor motioned to Niall and Caleb to join him outside the room where Alicia waited with a sleeping Beth in her lap.

"Well, she appears to have had a pretty good knock and doesn't remember much at this point. This is common with a head injury. I've seen the loss of memory last a few hours, a few days, or weeks. Sometimes, months pass before a patient recovers what they lost. In a few rare cases the memory never does return." Doc Minton's words weren't encouraging but needed to be said so they could decide how to proceed.

"She'll need a place to stay until her memory returns. Physically, she seems fine other than the head injury. But she can't go to the hotel and be left alone."

"Of course she can come out to the ranch with us. We've plenty of room and someone is around all the time," Alicia volunteered. She always seemed to be the first to offer help and the first to put the needs of others before her own. Doc Minton had counted on the woman's gracious nature.

"Wait a minute, Aunt Alicia. We can't go bringing a stranger into the house, someone we don't know. Think of Beth. Hell, we know nothing about this girl." Niall wasn't about to spend one more minute with someone who piqued his interest the way this stranger, Kate, seemed to. He'd felt it the day they met in Phoenix. The physical

47

awareness of her now made him uncomfortable. The idea of dealing with these feelings every day just didn't sit well with him.

A girl her age shouldn't be around a bunch of wild ranch hands who worked all week and spoke of not much else except how they planned to spend their Saturday nights—nights filled with whisky, cards, and bedding any willing female within their sight. He included his brothers, Drew and Will, in this group. Hell no. She was not coming back to the ranch.

"Okay, it's settled. We'll spend the night at Maria's and head back to the ranch early tomorrow," Alicia said, paying no attention to her nephew.

"Forget it, Aunt Alicia. Didn't you hear a word I said?" Niall couldn't contain his frustration.

"Of course, Niall," Alicia said, "but the last I checked, our agreement stated I handled anything concerning the house, and you handled anything concerning the cattle operations. Correct? Or did the rules change? Besides, where else will she go and have people around to check on her?"

Damn, but Alicia could be stubborn. Why now? "Fine, if that's what you want," Niall growled, "Doc, can you handle the two bodies?"

"Sure, Niall. I'll take good care of them and notify the sheriff in the morning." Doc smiled at the exchange between his long-time friends.

Within an hour, everyone, including Caleb, had rooms in Maria Alvarez's large home on the edge of town. A good night's rest was what they all needed before starting for the ranch in the morning.

49

Chapter Six

"I appreciate the offer, but I'd be intruding. Sounds like you already have a full house with your family and Kate." Alicia had offered Caleb a place at the ranch until he could make arrangements to travel on to California and the job he'd accepted. In his current state, the trip would be excruciating. Although not broken, he still had a hard time keeping his balance and supporting his weight.

"How about this?" Doc Minton offered. "There's a spare bedroom at my place you may use for a few weeks until your leg heals. Your being here will give me a chance to visit some out-of-the way ranches to check on things. You could tend to those who come to the clinic. What do you say?"

"The invitation is very generous, Doctor, but won't the townspeople get riled if they show up to find me and not you? I understand how small towns can be." Actually, Caleb liked the idea, maybe too much, and for possibly the wrong reasons.

"Tell you what," Doc Minton tried again. "I'll introduce you around over the next week and decide how folks take to you. May settle their minds to realize I believe you'll do fine when I'm out of the clinic. Sure would help me out a great deal, Caleb."

Caleb thought about it a minute before answering. "If you're positive, I'll accept." Caleb smiled. He didn't try to hide his pleasure. He would heal, practice a little medicine, and be close enough to visit Kate. From the minute she'd climbed into the stage, the woman had intrigued him. He couldn't seem to take his eyes off of her. She was cordial, but spoke little on the short trip out of Phoenix, preferring to worry the ring on her left hand. Interesting, but she introduced herself as Katherine, not Mrs. Someone, which would have been proper for a married woman. He'd like another chance to figure some things out.

"All right. With your living arrangements settled, Caleb, we'll be on our way out." Niall mounted Zeus for the ride home. "Someone will get word to one of you," he nodded toward the doctors, "if anything happens with the girl. Either Aunt Alicia or I will stop in on our trips to town to give you an update. I appreciate all you've done."

"Niall, I'm the one who is thankful for your assistance in the desert. Our fate changed considerably when you and your family rescued us." Caleb's sincerity got to Niall. He shook the hand offered to him and nodded.

This is going to be a long journey, Niall thought as they left the town limits. And he wasn't just referring to the trip back to the ranch.

******

"Hey, Niall, Aunt Alicia, Beth," Will called out from the front porch as the wagon pulled in front of the house. "Who's with you?"

Kate had drifted in and out of sleep for most of the ride. She now tried to sit up to squint at the person who asked the question. Her eyes fell on a younger version of Niall. He had different hair but the same strong features and keen eyes. She did a double take as another vision appeared. *Oh Lord, I must be in worse shape than I realized*, Kate thought as two of the same young man started down the porch.

"Hey, Aunt Alicia, what's going on?" Drew arrived first, with Will close on his heels.

"You can't seem to stack them up any faster, Niall? Now you're hauling them to the house in a wagon?" Will laughed as he offered his oldest brother a broad grin. He never missed a chance to taunt Niall. Fact is, he never missed a chance to tease most anyone, but, especially now, when most knew Niall was courting one woman while spending his Friday nights with another. Even though Niall controlled his temper most of the time, he wouldn't dismiss this challenge.

"Will and Drew, this is Kate. I don't know her last name and neither does she at the moment. She got injured in a stagecoach accident near Watsonville. Doc checked her over and Aunt Alicia volunteered a room with us until she gets her memory back. That's the entire story. Either of you have anything else to say?"

"Uh, no, Niall, I'm good," Drew ventured. Niall was riled and Drew wanted no part of a skirmish between Will and their oldest brother.

"Fine with me, Niall." Will offered his hand to Kate when she looked up at the twins. "Would you like some help to the house, ma'am?"

They're twins, she realized. "Yes, thank you. Will, is it?" Kate asked as she took his hand.

"Yes, ma'am, and this is Drew. As you can see, we're twins, but I'm the smarter one, braver and faster, too," Will's smile broadened. Kate couldn't help but grin at Will's attempt at positioning himself apart from his twin.

"Yeah, but I'm older by at least two minutes, so when Niall's gone, I'm in charge." Drew smiled at his twin and helped Will lift Kate out of the wagon.

"Kate will be in the office for a few days until she's good to climb stairs. She'll move up to Jamie's old room when she's ready." Alicia guided Kate inside as the boys brought in a couple of trunks reclaimed from the accident. Thank goodness they had a big house.

The first thing Kate noticed as they entered the office was the size—it was spacious with a large desk and leather chair, two guest chairs, a sofa, and a good-sized fireplace. One wall had a floor to ceiling bookcase. The last wall caught her eye, as it contained three large windows, positioned with an unobstructed view of the barn and stables.

"What a wonderful room, Alicia. So large and, well, beautiful," Kate commented.

"Why, thank you, Kate. This was my late husband's office. It's Niall's now," Alicia held up her hand when she noticed Kate start to object. "And don't worry about being in his way. I expect you'll be out of this room in a day or two and in the bedroom upstairs," Alicia said as she helped Kate get settled on the daybed.

"Is your husband in this picture, Alicia?" Kate indicated a framed photograph next to the daybed.

"Yes, Stuart is in the center. Niall is on his left, Jamie next to him, and the twins next to me on the other side. Everyone looks so happy, don't you think? How did we know so much would change over the next several years?" Alicia spoke almost to herself rather than Kate.

"Jamie?"

"Oh, yes. Jamie is three years younger than Niall. He's a U.S. Marshal now. Followed in the steps of a good friend of all of ours. We don't see much of him, but I sure do miss him." Her voice had grown quiet and Alicia turned away, as if to inspect the room again. "Anyway, my bedroom is right next door if you need me."

"Alicia, thank you for taking me into your home. I'm not sure what I'd do without your help." Kate felt overwhelmed, sore, and was nursing a raging headache. She was also surprised this woman would take her in without questions and over the objections of Niall. It appeared he ran the ranch operations and Alicia the house. She wondered about many things concerning this family including Beth's mother. Where was she? But it was too much to think about now, she decided. First, she needed sleep. She also required time to regain her memory, and figure out why her travels brought her to Arizona.

"Honey, we're glad you're here. You just need to rest. I'm sure your memory will return soon. Don't you worry, someone is in the house most all the time, and if not, they're a short distance away. We'll get you settled and I'll start dinner." Alicia was efficient, with an abundance of energy, which made Kate feel even more tired. All Kate could think about now was sleep.

******

"What are we going to do with her, Niall? Has anyone thought to go through her things to learn anything about her? I don't like having strange people around with access to the house, the barn, and your family." Gus Dixon had been on the ranch since just after Niall's Uncle Stuart took it over.

Tall and lean, his skin was cracked like well-used leather, his disposition equally as tough. He had married twice and buried both wives without ever having children. Niall, Jamie, Drew, and Will were like his own and Gus was fiercely protective of them, as well as Alicia and Beth. As the ranch foreman, he partnered with Pete Cantlin, the chief wrangler, to hire and fire the men. Gus had trained many of them. He'd signed up with Stuart soon after resigning his position with the U.S. Marshals Service. Niall trusted both men with his life and those of his family.

"Hell, Gus, I understand how you feel, but there's just no reasoning with Alicia about this. She's made up her mind, and the girl is staying here until she's regained her memory. Alicia went through her trunks and found nothing but a bible inscribed to Katherine. No other family information. One trunk had opened when it crashed to the ground during the accident. Some clothing and papers scattered in the wind. Perhaps there was more in her companion's trunk, but the wagon was full and we had to leave it behind. Besides, we were set on getting the passengers to Fire Mountain for medical help. I plan to contact the stage office in Phoenix, in case they know anything else about her. From what I know, they don't get much information on passengers. They sell seats and get people on their way." Niall wasn't pleased with the situation and had been in a foul mood since their return. Something about Kate set him on edge. He had plans in place for his and Beth's future. His instincts, which rarely failed him, told him this stranger posed a threat to everything.

Chapter Seven

Only a few days had passed since Kate arrived at the MacLaren ranch. Days with little progress as far as regaining her memory, but significant progress with her physical health. By the end of her second day, she was bored and begging Alicia to let her help with chores. At first, Alicia refused, but then decided it best to have Kate help out with the hope it would trigger memories.

Kate found she loved to cook and prepared many dishes by heart. She didn't remember when or where she'd learned them, but it gave her satisfaction to know she had useful skills tucked away in her head.

Alicia discovered that their guest was well educated. The books found in her trunks, plus the way she spoke and acted, indicated she'd been well schooled, and was, perhaps, from a more refined home. She stayed calm and gracious, even when it was apparent to everyone she was frustrated with her lack of ability to remember her last name, her family, her birthplace––anything. The wedding ring Kate wore seemed to be the one indication there might be people searching for her. It was a simple gold band with a small inscription, nothing spectacular to indicate she came from wealth.

Kate struggled, trying to regain her memory while the same questions pounded in her head day after day. Who was her husband? Did she have children? Why was she traveling with a companion instead of her husband? Where was she headed? If she and her companion had spoken more of themselves to the other passengers, someone might have remembered something that would help her, but, according to Caleb, both had sat silent after boarding the stage and making brief introductions.

******

"Miss Kate, read me another story," Beth pleaded after dinner on Friday night. Her father hadn't stayed long after finishing the meal. He had saddled Zeus and ridden into town with a couple of the other ranch hands. Alicia said he'd had the same routine for the last few weeks. Work the ranch during the week, relax in town on Friday night, take care of business on Saturday, and return home before supper. Sunday everyone attended church. Niall and Beth stayed in town for dinner with Mrs. van Deelin on recent Sundays, leaving Alicia to ride back to the ranch with Gus or another ranch hand. The schedule appeared to be the same for this weekend.

"Of course, Beth, I'd be happy to read you a story. What would you like to hear?" Kate loved kids and wondered if she might have been a teacher or a governess before the accident. It was apparent to everyone she had the skills to run a household, as well as the temperament to handle most situations. Losing her memory and living with a household of total strangers hadn't changed her basic nature.

"Read the one about the knight and princess. You remember? He is kind of mean but she is beautiful and nice. I like that one the best." Beth's enthusiasm for everything made life at the ranch so much more bearable. Like all children, she wasn't perfect, but she was always excited about something, and laughed a good deal of the time. *Could I have a daughter like her waiting for me to return?* The not-knowing was driving Kate crazy. And Niall, he was also driving her crazy. He seldom spoke to her. When he did his tone was one of tolerance, not one of welcome. Regardless, she was drawn to him. She hadn't known him until he stopped for the accident, but something about Niall made her feel they had met before. He seemed familiar, but she couldn't place why.

She was always struck by his height and strong build. He wore his black hair somewhat longer than most men. Kate had noticed that, in the light, it had streaks of dark purple, almost the color of blackberries. But his bright green eyes, the greenest eyes she'd ever seen, seemed to draw her in. When he glanced in her direction she felt odd, as if she'd been in this same situation with him before—staring at him and feeling nervous, a little excited or scared—she wasn't sure which. But even if she couldn't remember, she knew these were not good feelings to have, especially if, like her gold band implied, she was married.

******

"Another, Gloria."

"Sure thing, Niall." Gloria Chalmette had known Niall since he was old enough to come into the Desert Dove Saloon with his uncle. Stuart was never one to avail himself of anything but the liquor and occasional card game, but Niall had no ties. At twenty, he had experienced one night with Gloria, and had never requested anyone else. Gloria found Niall to be a meticulous lover. He never left until she'd experienced as much pleasure as she'd given him. Except during his brief marriage, it was well known that Gloria made herself available to him whenever he came to the Dove, as locals called it. She'd owned the saloon since she was twenty-three, and was a year younger than Niall. They were good friends as well as casual lovers.

"Leave the bottle, Gloria."

She winced at the last statement. Niall was never one to use alcohol as a way to ponder his troubles, or even celebrate successes. He drank to wash down the dust and be social, not to numb his senses.

"If that's what you want, Niall. But I can think of other ways to kill time, if that's what you're doing."

"Maybe later. For now, just leave me and the bottle to ourselves." Niall knew he was being rude to someone who was only looking out for him, but right now he didn't care.

"Mr. MacLaren, may I join you?"

Niall glanced up to see Sam Browning, the other passenger in the fatal stage wreck, approach and order a whiskey. He looked better. His arm was still bandaged, but the cuts and bruises on his face were healed. Niall realized for the first time that Sam was older than he first thought. Plus, he was wearing the badge of a deputy.

"Sam, good to see you. I wondered where you went after we found the doctor. Appears you've

60

settled in fast, by the deputy's badge you're wearing."

"That's why I was coming to Fire Mountain. Sheriff Rawlins offered me a job the last time he was in Phoenix. I finally accepted. Once we got to town, I thought it best to report the accident."

Sam had learned much about Niall from talking with the sheriff. Niall was one of those considered a town leader, had a standing arrangement with Gloria, kept to himself, had lost his wife years ago, was considered a fair boss. And it was rumored that he was courting Mrs. van Deelin, a widow of twenty-five, whom Rawlins said owned a good-sized piece of land north of town, and a small mansion in town. Sam also learned that Niall was the older brother of his friend, Jamie MacLaren. Lawmen tended to get to know other lawmen. Jamie MacLaren was one of the best.

"How's your houseguest doing?" Sam sounded casual, but Niall thought he picked up something more. Or maybe he just imagined it. Sam's question irked Niall, and damned if he knew why. Simple question, simple answer, but that didn't change the fact that Niall wanted nothing more than to forget about his houseguest, not talk about her.

"Fine. She's doing fine." Niall's tone was final and Sam chose to change the subject.

He turned so his elbows rested on the bar with his eyes scanning the saloon. About thirty men were present, which was a little light for a Friday. Many Sam had already met. Some were townspeople and others from local ranches.

Then there was Gloria Chalmette. Now that was one fine-looking woman. She wore her chestnut brown hair swept off her face and held with a comb that allowed long, tightly curled tendrils to fall over her shoulders. Gloria's eyes were the golden color of melted caramel, and her figure—well, his mind didn't need to go in that direction. A shame she belonged to Niall.

"We've been getting reports of stolen property— cash, jewelry, nothing significant—but four complaints so far. Three from houses in town and one from Jacobson."

That got Niall's attention. "John's place was robbed?"

"That's right. A few hundred dollars from his desk. He kept it for emergencies. Also, some jewelry kept in a trunk upstairs. The thing is, John says he always locks his desk, and there was no damage." Sam kept his voice low, barely above a whisper. "The three robberies in town were coins and some jewelry. Strange. The robber only took a little from each house. Might not have been noticed if one neighbor hadn't mentioned it to the next. They checked their houses and found items missing. They mentioned it to another neighbor, and damned if they didn't have a few things missing, too. I expect we're going to hear about more."

Niall thought it over, but nothing made much sense. "Could be kids, but what would they do with jewelry? And why take the risk of robbing someone and leaving other valuables behind?"

Sam had to agree. "Well, be aware of it and let the sheriff or me know if you notice anything missing, or anyone someplace they shouldn't be. So you know, we're checking on all the newcomers."

Niall scowled at that. "Does that include Kate?"

"Everyone," Sam said before pushing away from the bar and walking out the door.

******

"You heard anything about robberies in town, Gloria?" Niall was sitting up in bed with one arm bent behind his head, nursing a whiskey while Gloria stretched, pulled on her robe, and made her way to the vanity.

"No, not a thing. You heard something?" Robberies or theft of any kind were rare in Fire Mountain.

"The new deputy, Sam Browning, mentioned it tonight. He said they were paying particular attention to newcomers."

"Including your new house guest?" Gloria looked over her shoulder as she brushed her long hair. She was a beautiful woman, exotic in a way, with cream-tinted skin. Her face was smooth, absent of the heavy powders and rouges so common to those she employed. Gloria almost never wore lip color as her lips were a luscious cherry. She made enough money to order the best lotions from the east and used them morning and night in the dry Arizona climate. Her skin was as soft as butter and Niall loved touching her––all over. Tonight had been no exception.

There was a hint of something in Gloria's voice, but Niall was too relaxed to question it. "Yes, including our houseguest. Don't see any connection there. She hasn't been off the ranch since she arrived a few days ago, but I guess they need to check out everyone."

"Well, the sheriff is thorough when something gets his hackles up, and it's no coincidence he'd hire a deputy who feels the same. Sam seems like a decent guy. Maybe he'll stay longer than the last two." Gloria made sure she had good relationships with the sheriff and his men. Never knew when you would need their help. And Sam, well, he gave her girls something to stare at, dream about. He wasn't handsome, not in the classic sense, but his rugged good-looks, tall, lean frame, warm brown skin, black hair, and silver blue eyes gave him the appearance of a man who had no trouble attracting woman.

"It's just curious, is all. A little money and some jewelry, small batches that might not have been noticed, but were. Something for you to be aware of." Niall swung his legs off the bed and grabbed his clothes.

"Not staying, I take it?" Gloria asked as he continued to dress.

"Not tonight, darl'n. I have things at home that need to be taken care of first thing, and I don't have other business in town right now. Next time I'll plan to say all night." Niall didn't know why he felt compelled to head back tonight. He had nothing pressing, but he felt restless and needed to be on the move.

Gloria placed her brush back on the vanity, stood, and watched him strap on his gun. He was the best man she'd ever known. They'd been seeing each other for so long that she sometimes forgot he wasn't hers. Never would be. If her life had turned out different perhaps they would've had a chance. Circumstances had set her on this path long before she'd met Niall. They were good together. "Next time then, Niall." Gloria walked him to the door, wrapped her arms around his neck, and gave him a long kiss. "Next time."

Chapter Eight

It surprised Kate to see Niall at the breakfast table Saturday morning with Will, Drew, and Beth. She'd understood he seldom returned home on Saturday until right before the evening meal.

"Good morning, Kate. How was your night?" Alicia asked as Kate sat down to fill her plate with eggs and a biscuit. She noticed that the bags under the young woman's eyes were beginning to fade, and her color had improved over the last week.

"Much better, Alicia. No dreams, at least not that I can recall," Kate answered between bites. Alicia was a great cook and she seemed to know the exact amount to make so that nothing went to waste.

"Kate? I'd like to speak with you after breakfast, if you have the time." All eyes landed on Kate. Niall wasn't making a request and everyone knew it.

"Of course, Mr. MacLaren. I'm not very hungry, so now is fine, if you're finished." Kate's stomach growled as she spoke, even though her hunger had died with his words. She'd wondered how long it would take Niall to convince Alicia it was time their houseguest found other lodging. She wasn't surprised, but had no idea where she'd go or how she'd live. Fact was, Kate was scared. There had been no money, no banking information, and no hint of her final destination in the belongings they were able to salvage from the scattered wreckage. Kate wished they'd taken Mrs. Stelford's luggage from the stage, but with the injuries, everyone had been in a hurry to reach Fire Mountain. Niall sent men back to fetch it, but by then everything had vanished, and along with it, any clues to her identity.

Five minutes later Kate found herself facing Niall, who sat behind his desk in the office. It was a good-sized piece of furniture, about three feet from the front to the back, behind which Niall relaxed in his chair and focused his gaze on her. Somehow Kate still felt crowded. She backed away slowly, so slowly she hadn't noticed until Niall grinned at her. "You don't need to flee from me, Kate. I'm not known for assaulting young women." Niall's thoughts flew to their encounter in Phoenix, and watched to see if there was any reaction from his guest. There was none.

"No, of course not. Was there something you wanted to talk about?" Kate's voiced sounded strained, even to her own ears.

"Please, sit down. I don't believe this will take long." For some perverse reason, Niall was enjoying Kate's discomfiture. She sat, but her back was rigid in the large leather chair, and she had to scoot forward so her feet touched the floor. Her hands were folded in her lap as she rubbed the golden band on her left hand between the thumb and index finger of her right hand.

"It's been almost a week since the accident. From what Aunt Alicia has said, you still don't remember much. Tell me, do you remember anything about yourself, your life?" Niall had a hard time believing they still knew nothing about Kate.

"Not much." Sadness laced her voice. "At times I sense or feel that I'm going to remember something, but I don't. Alicia made a pie and the smell triggered something so strong I had to sit down. Nothing stuck. An image, or shadow of a face, flashes through my mind, but it's gone in an instant." Her head lowered as her shoulders drooped at the complete lack of any memory. A deep sigh fell from her lips before she continued. "The same thing happened yesterday when Gus and Pete rode up to the barn. The image of a man on a horse appeared, almost like a vision, and then was gone, but a memory stuck. It became quite clear to me that I know how to ride. Not just sit a horse and stay on, but ride. Fast, hard, all-out."

She stopped to take a ragged breath. Discussing this with Niall was tougher than she would have thought. Maybe talking about it would help ease the anxious feeling that was her constant companion. "Yesterday I was working in the garden with Alicia when a rattler appeared. I went for Alicia's rifle and shot the snake before Alicia had time to turn and reach for the gun. When that happened, my mind drifted, and I saw the shadow of a large man with broad shoulders, and a rifle resting in his right hand. The man started to turn toward me. I tried so hard to keep the image turning so I could see him, but it was gone in an instant." The clear defeat in Kate's voice pierced at something inside Niall, a feeling he thought long gone. "I'm sorry, Mr. MacLaren. I know this is a disappointment to you. Having a stranger in your home must be hard, and I won't think less of you if you ask me to leave."

The last gave Niall pause. Yes, he'd wished her gone. Kate distracted him, raised unwelcomed feelings. No matter what he felt, tossing her out didn't sit well with him. "Well, it appears there are some things we need to discuss."

"All right."

"First, Aunt Alicia tells me you've been spending a lot of time with Beth—reading to her, working with her on numbers and writing," Niall began.

Kate rushed to explain. "Alicia assured me it would be okay. She said I was not over-stepping my bounds. I can stop if you'd rather I not work with her. It's just, I sense I'm good at this, that I've done it before, teaching I mean. And Beth is such a quick learner. So incredibly bright for being so young..." Niall held up his hand to stop her, and let her catch a breath.

"Kate," Niall said in a calming voice, "I have no issue with you teaching Beth. Aunt Alicia has asked me to consider hiring you to be Beth's governess. She has a lot to do as one of the ranch owners. With all the house duties and added ranch chores, she worries about having enough time for Beth. She gets tired and can't always keep up. Beth needs someone who can school her, guide her about the things young girls are supposed to know." Niall stopped to gauge Kate's interest. She stared at him, although her eyes started to tear as he continued.

"It's no secret that I haven't wanted you here. I know nothing about you, and now Aunt Alicia wants me to trust you to guide my daughter. Although there's been nothing negative in your behavior, how do I know you'll have the right influence on her?

How do I know she'll be safe with you? Why should I give you this job when there are at least a couple of women in town who would make an excellent governess for Beth?"

"Mrs. van Deelin being one?" Kate knew the minute the words were out that she'd made a mistake. Why did she have to share so much of what spilled into her head?

Niall, who'd turned to stare out the window, snapped his head around. "Mrs. van Deelin has no place in this conversation. She is someone you and I will never discuss. Do you understand?"

Kate swallowed hard, but stared straight into his eyes and nodded her head in understanding.

Although Niall had no intention of ever talking about his relationship with Jocelyn, or any other woman, he admired Kate's ability to withstand his scrutiny and not cower like so many women might. "What I want to know, Katherine," his voice hardened somewhat, "is whether you'd like to be considered for this position, and why I should consider giving it to you."

It was the first time he'd called her by her proper name since her arrival. She'd made a serious error. She wanted to be Beth's governess and remain at the ranch. Stay near Niall. *Near Niall*? What had brought that on? Kate was never one to delude herself. Each time she was around Niall she felt alive, nervous, hopeful, scared, and many other things she didn't understand.

"Mr. MacLaren. I apologize if my brash comment about Mrs. van Deelin was out of line. Of course you are right that your personal life is none of my business. Yes, I do want the position," she insisted. "I cannot say how I know, but teaching and working with children seems to be quite natural for me. It would be an honor to be Beth's governess. I hope you believe I would never do anything to harm her, or anyone else in your family. There are no other assurances to offer you, except that I would rather harm myself than any of them."

Niall didn't miss the sincerity in her words. Kate's behavior since she'd arrived had shown she was warm-hearted, kind, and quick to help without being asked. She seemed to sense what needed to get done and jumped right in. A part of him, a large part, had hoped she'd decline the position. Each time he looked at her, he saw the pretty, blonde woman, whose dazzling blue eyes swept over him in open admiration, on the street in Phoenix. But more disconcerting, he saw a woman he wanted more than any he'd met since Camille. And that was not acceptable. She was a distraction, a serious distraction. He had a plan, goals for him, Beth, the ranch, and Kate played no part in these plans.

"Mr. MacLaren?" It had been so long that Kate thought he might not have heard her.

Niall shook off his thoughts and addressed Kate in a clipped voice. "All right, we will give it a month and see how it goes. You will receive room, board, and a wage. If you regain your memory during this time, you may decide how to proceed. Likewise, a month gives me time to assess your skills and decide if you are the right match for Beth. Agreed?"

"Yes, agreed, Mr. MacLaren. I appreciate the offer." Kate took a slow, deep breath and started to leave.

"Wait, there is another issue I wish to discuss."

She sat back into her chair and waited for Niall to continue.

"Since you have been having these 'thoughts' or 'visions,' I think we should explore them. I suggest we go riding. Test some of your theories. See if these visions from your past are real or if they're dead-ends to ignore." Niall doubted Kate would show the slightest aptitude for either riding or shooting, but at least it was something they could do to help her regain her memory.

"When?"

"Today, now, unless you have other plans." Niall preferred to get this over with then find Gus and Pete to discuss the recent robberies.

"Now is fine. Shall I meet you at the barn in a few minutes?" Kate was excited and wanted to latch onto this offer before he changed his mind.

"Fifteen minutes at the barn."

******

The ride felt less and less like a good idea about ten minutes away from the house. Kate sat her horse like a veteran rider. She'd chosen a horse and had it saddled by the time Niall walked into the barn. She hadn't picked the one Niall thought best. He would've chosen Daisy, a twelve-year-old mare about fourteen-and-a-half hands, even-tempered and easy to handle.

Instead, Kate had chosen Captain, an eight-year-old gelding over fifteen hands. Pete had trained Captain. He was fast but sure-footed, feisty but responded well to commands, excellent with cattle, and strong. Pete had packed him for hunting trips as well as taken him for long rides over the ranch. He was a beautiful sorrel with a white blaze, white stockings, black mane, and black tail. Niall had to admit that Kate looked stunning astride him. And that thought brought back the real reason for his distress at this outing.

She wore a split riding skirt that fit her as tight as a glove. Camille had always ridden sidesaddle, but not Kate. She'd walked up to Captain, secured the reins while grabbing his main with her left hand, fit her boot in the stirrup, steadied herself with her right hand, and hoisted herself up in one, smooth movement, the skirt clinging to her beautifully rounded backside. "Christ," he growled under his breath.

They were approaching a small hill when Niall nudged Zeus into an easy canter. Kate followed a few yards behind, relaxing into the steady pace. She reined in Captain next to Niall as he stopped at the crest.

"We'll head west across that meadow, and visit parts of the ranch before we use the guns." He secured his hat. "Try to keep up." The last was said with a slight smirk as Niall turned and sent Zeus down the hill into the meadow, and then let loose.

The rider and horse made a magnificent image Kate observed as she moved Captain forward to catch up to Zeus. Niall sat straight and had excellent control. He was one of those men born to ride, born to control, and from what she'd seen, born to lead. Today, however, was about Kate, and she aimed to surprise him.

Kate knew she'd catch Niall if Captain rose to the challenge. Her horse moved out and took his cues from Kate. Before long they were a few short yards behind Niall, who hadn't bothered to glance back for several seconds. Kate wondered if his arrogance would keep him from acknowledging her skills. She pushed deeper into the saddle and leaned forward over Captain's neck. The horse was pure pleasure. Kate's connection to the animal had been instantaneous. She approached Zeus's hindquarters and wondered if Niall would allow her to ride Captain after today.

Niall glanced over his left shoulder to see Kate laughing as she gained on him. Zeus had a lot more in him, but Niall was more interested in what Kate could do, and so far she was doing superb. He knew Zeus and he knew Captain. There wasn't a chance that Captain could outrun his horse, but he didn't want to end the race so soon. Instead, he allowed Kate to come up close. For a hundred yards they paced each other, Kate relaxed and in complete control. A few minutes later, with one subtle command from Niall, Zeus shot out, flying across the valley.

Kate knew she could never catch them. She slowed Captain and enjoyed the sight of Niall and his animal moving as one.

Chapter Nine

Niall didn't know what he'd expected from Kate that morning, but it hadn't been that she could ride or handle his Colt better than many men. She was more than competent at both. The woman was smart, funny, gracious, even-tempered, and accepted all that had been handed to her since the accident. Why wasn't someone looking for her? Where was her husband? Alicia had commented that the wedding band she wore included an inscription that read, "Love, T."

Niall reflected on what he'd learned. The stage company had no record about next of kin. The ticket agent did remember the women discussing Los Angeles, but nothing more. Most people walked in, paid cash for a ticket, and boarded the stage. No other information was required. The company didn't care about names or identities. Pay cash and get on your way.

For a brief period while shooting, Kate had another image. She'd told Niall it appeared to be the same tall man with broad shoulders. He still held a rifle in his right hand but this time he wore a hat, just like Niall's. Something glittered on his belt as the image turned towards her. An instant later, the image vanished. Niall could feel her frustration at not being able to pull the image in, make it mean something, anything that could give her some hope her memory was returning.

"You think she's faking it?" Gus asked as they walked back to the barn after dinner. He, Pete, and

Niall planned to check out the bunkhouse, barn, and house to see if they spotted anything unusual. Even though Sam had said the robberies consisted of cash and jewelry, Niall wanted everything checked. He had an unknown woman living in his home without a memory. Now there had been a series of robberies. She could ride and shoot, which weren't unusual out here, but her abilities were well above average. Could there be a connection? No. He instantly dismissed the thought as nonsense. Niall wasn't one to be easily duped, but as far as he was concerned, there was no possible way Kate could be involved.

"Don't see how she could be. She hasn't left the ranch except to go to town with Alicia. You should see her, Gus, when she almost catches a memory, then loses it. It shakes her up pretty bad. Doc says it's a matter of time at this point. Says the visions are an indication her memory is trying to break free, which is a positive sign. It can't come soon enough for me."

"Seems the two of you are getting on okay now," Pete interjected, but paused when he saw Niall give him a questioning look. "You know, with you hiring her to teach Beth, it seems that you've at least begun to speak to her. You know, full sentences and all." This was said with a slight smile.

Niall let the comment pass. "You know as well as I do that it was Alicia's idea to hire her on. I still don't want her here. She's a complication, and none of us needs more complications." Niall didn't seem to catch what he was saying, but Gus and Pete looked at each other and grinned.

"What?" Niall asked when he saw their faces.

"Nothing, Boss, just agreeing that no one needs more complications, especially female." Pete and Gus were still smiling as they headed toward the back corral.

******

The next few days passed with no new images. Beth loved to learn, and took to Kate's teaching with an eagerness that surprised her governess. Most of the time Alicia had to interrupt them for dinner, but that was fine with Niall, as his daughter was thriving. Kate even began to teach Beth how to play the piano. Stuart had bought one for Alicia years ago, but she seldom played since her husband's death, and no one else knew how, until Kate arrived. She played every day and Beth had worn her down by begging for lessons.

Niall's real concern was that his daughter was becoming too attached to her governess. He wondered what would happen when Kate's memory returned. Perhaps she'd leave. Wouldn't bother him, he told himself, but it might be devastating for Beth.

Nevertheless, he had no time to dwell on Kate. Saturday was his daughter's seventh birthday. Alicia had invited every child around to help Beth celebrate. Food was being prepared and games planned. *Seven, how had it gone by so fast?* God, how he wished Camille could be here to see it.

Camille. He'd thought about her quite a bit the last couple of weeks. For the last few years he'd found himself thinking of her a couple times a week. Thoughts of her now occupied his mind more often. Perhaps he felt guilt for trying to move on and leave the past behind. Funny, he never felt guilty when he was with Gloria or visiting Jocelyn. The first time he was with Gloria after Camille died, he felt as if he'd betrayed his wife. It had been at least two years at that point, but he still felt the pang of guilt. Niall had to think his growing attraction to Kate accounted for part of it. But he'd loved Camille, and he didn't love Kate. Didn't believe he could ever love again.

Kate. He refused to think of her as anything more than a short-term guest, a governess for Beth, but she was the most fascinating woman he'd ever met. He didn't understand his fierce attraction to her. She had every quality he would want if he were searching for a true mate, someone he could love, cherish. But he wasn't interested in those things any longer. Those needs died with Camille.

Jocelyn. Even though she had sold most of her holdings, she still owned one good-sized measure of pastureland that abutted one corner of the MacLaren ranch. The grazing land was excellent, and there was an abundance of water. Combined, their lands would increase his holdings and further the goal to own the largest spread in the northern section of the territory. Jocelyn had the land and water to enlarge his spread, and ensure a future for Beth. She'd offered to sell it to him, and that's when the idea of marrying her had taken shape. In Niall's mind, the most important asset Jocelyn would bring to a marriage would be her substantial political connections. He wasn't in love with her, never would be, and he knew she didn't love him, but together they'd make a good partnership. He didn't need her money, but the fact that she had considerable wealth was no deterrent. And she'd made it clear in the last several months that she wanted him. She admired his intellect, solid business sense, commitment, and his drive to grow the ranch. She'd told him more than once that he was the toughest man she'd ever met. And that, in a nutshell, was what she wanted—a tough, rugged westerner to hang on her arm and warm her bed.

No, he didn't love Jocelyn. Hell, he didn't know if he even liked her much. But she knew about Gloria, and accepted the fact that he wouldn't stop seeing her if Jocelyn married him. It would be a marriage to satisfy each other's selfish interests, not of the heart, and it was the right thing to do. At least, that was what he told himself each time he was around Kate, and when he saw Jocelyn. It was the right thing for the ranch, for him, for Beth.

Chapter Ten

Niall shrugged into his grey chambray shirt, tucked it into his tight-in-all-the-right-places pants, secured his gun belt, and knelt over the bed to deliver a quick peck on Gloria's cheek before leaving. She liked watching him dress. She pretended to be asleep so that he wouldn't suspect how much she enjoyed looking him over. He had stayed the night, but they'd spent as much time talking as anything else. Although each had plans that did not include the other, their friendship was close, and they had a history of seeking advice from the other when facing difficult decisions.

"Don't know why the rush, Niall. I understand your plans, but consider how they'll affect Beth. It's no secret that Jocelyn doesn't like children and refused to have them with her husband. She prefers the social life to family life." Gloria had repeated this in various ways, several times, over the last few weeks, and at least twice tonight, between what had turned out to be intense, almost desperate sex.

"I don't care if Jocelyn does or doesn't like Beth, as she'll have no influence on how I raise my daughter. I will bed her, but there are no plans for children, so I don't care about her feelings on that subject. What I do care about is her land, and social standing back east. Her connections could be critical as the territory grows. As the widow of someone who was considered part of the industrial elite, her circle includes some highly influential people, people the MacLaren's could benefit from knowing." His logic was becoming more and more difficult to defend. Any enthusiasm he'd once had for bedding Jocelyn had diminished significantly as his mind continued to wander to thoughts of Kate. The spoken words told the story of a man committed to a marriage without love. His mind and heart kept interrupting the ending, nagging at him to reconsider what he once thought of as the perfect future for him and his family.

"Even so, just having that woman around Beth would scare the hell out of me. Her actions will still influence someone so young and impressionable, even if you don't allow her any input on how Beth is raised. As for her social circle, she can turn those friends of hers into enemies of yours in less time than it takes my girls to complete one round up and down the stairs. Don't think for a moment that Jocelyn won't insert herself into the lives of everyone at the ranch, and it won't be a pretty sight, especially if her machinations are aimed at your family."

Those last words haunted Niall during the entire ride home. Gloria wasn't one to jump to hasty conclusions, and never let emotions cloud her judgment. She had a generous heart, but Gloria Chalmette was no pushover. Plus, she was in a position to see and hear things he wasn't. Tomorrow was Sunday, and another dinner with Jocelyn. These dinners had become an obligation, part of his plan, not something that he anticipated with any pleasure. After Gloria's observations, he knew it would be wise to focus more on the woman he was courting instead of her connections and property.

*****

Niall arrived at the ranch late Saturday morning, as Alicia put the final pie on the rack to cool. Kate supervised the birthday decorations being hung by several ranch hands. Pete directed others to clean up around the front of the house and set up tables.

"So, how's Gloria doing?" Will asked, loud enough for Kate to hear, as he grabbed the reins of Niall's horse to lead Zeus into the barn. Will just couldn't let Niall's Friday nights go by without a dig. Most of the other men, including his brother, Drew, never mentioned his visits with Gloria, but Will enjoyed provoking Niall.

Anger flashed in Niall's green eyes. "Don't go there, Will," he warned in a tight, but controlled, voice. He was in no mood to discuss his nights with Gloria, and didn't want the subject brought up in front of Kate. He'd noticed her wince when Will mentioned Gloria. She'd stared at the two for a moment before turning to go back into the house. Niall was pretty sure she knew what his Fridays in town meant, but for some reason he felt bad about being with Gloria when he looked at Kate.

"Hell, Niall. Maybe you shouldn't be going *there* when the whole town knows you're courting Mrs. van Deelin." Will said this last over his shoulder as he walked into the barn.

That was enough. In a few long strides Niall caught up with his younger brother, grabbed him by the collar, and tossed him against the barn wall.

"That's enough, Will. What I do with Gloria, or Jocelyn, is none of your business. You say something like that again and I'll do more than shove you against the wall, you got that?" Niall spoke in a low voice, but his words were chilling. Niall had never punched either of the twins, but he was on the verge of unleashing now. Will could see it, and made a quick decision to back off.

"Yeah, I got it." Will pushed himself away from Niall, muttering something about stupid-ass, blind, older brothers, and headed to the shed.

Niall stood there, taking deep breaths to calm his temper, staring after Will, and wondering what had just happened. He never threatened his brothers. Well, except Jamie. He and Jamie had always been at odds. That was one of the reasons Jamie had found it necessary to leave the ranch a few years ago and strike out on his own. An argument about a woman had triggered the final blow-up. Niall still felt the loss, and hoped that, one day, they could lay aside their differences, so Jamie would return to take his place on the ranch.

But this, today, with Will, was different. The mention of Gloria in front of Kate had set him off in a way that was unexpected. Will had thrown this same thing at Niall before, and they'd been able to laugh about it. But Kate had never been present.

Niall understood Will. He knew his brother had strong values and didn't grasp how Niall could court one woman and bed another. Niall didn't know if Will had ever had a woman, but guessed not. His brother had focused on one female for years, Emily Jacobson, and Niall suspected they'd marry someday. He tried to make allowances for his brother's lack of experience. Will didn't know what

83

it was like to love someone so much that no other woman could take her place. Nor did he understand the physical needs a man still had, even after losing her. There was no chance Will would be able to comprehend why Niall would choose to marry without love. Instead, Will taunted and teased him about the two women. The teasing had been a source of play before Kate had arrived. Now, it had become something much more serious. It had to stop.

His activities were no longer a topic Niall wanted brought up in public, especially in front of Kate. But why not? Why did he care what Kate, most likely a married woman, thought about his Friday nights with Gloria? Hell, he didn't care what anyone thought about it, and most of the town, the men anyway, knew about Gloria, and Jocelyn. But it did nag at him as he reflected on the three women.

He felt safe with Gloria, comfortable, with no demands. He looked forward to his Fridays, their talks and time in bed, as well as his ease at being able to walk away without regrets. With Jocelyn, he felt different. She was a duty, nothing more. Although he found her attractive, and he did plan to consummate their marriage, there was no chemistry, no warmth, and no sense of attachment other than how a possible marriage benefited each other. But with Kate, he saw everything he wanted in a woman—a woman his family had taken to without reservation, who touched him in some way each time he was around her. Unfortunately, she was the one woman not available to him. The gold band she wore was all the proof he needed.

******

"Papa, come and help me with my presents. I can't lift this one." Beth had the one he, Drew, and Will had gone together to buy. It weighed as much as she did, but she still tried to push it into the center of the circle created by all the eager kids who watched.

"Hold on a minute, squirt, I'll get it." Drew strolled up and lifted the package without effort, depositing it smack in the middle of the circle. "There you go. It's all yours."

Beth clapped her hands then attacked the paper. What she found was the prettiest saddle she had ever seen in all of her seven years. It was bigger than her other saddle. This one had scrollwork where her first one was plain, and her name was tooled on one side, roses on the other. She loved it.

"Papa, Papa, thank you. I love it!"

"Sweetheart, it's from your uncles and me, all combined, so you need to thank both of them, too." Niall watched as Beth jumped into Drew's arms for a hug, then ran over to Will and did the same.

"Can we put it on Misty? All the kids could try it." Her excitement was contagious.

"Sure, Beth, I'll bring out your horse so we can give the saddle a try." Niall started into the barn but found Kate, already inside, putting a bridle on Misty. She'd sensed what his daughter would want before he had, and for some reason that aggravated him.

"I'll get her." Niall knew his voice sounded curt.

"Oh, it's all right, I have her." Kate smiled at him as she started to walk past with Misty.

Niall moved to block her path. "I said I'll take her out to Beth. You can go busy yourself with the other ladies. This isn't part of your job." Niall didn't know what the hell was wrong with him. He sounded like a jerk. Kate just stood staring at him. His words hurt. He could see it in her eyes and posture. Niall noticed her throat working, like she wanted to say something, but instead she handed over the reins and started to turn back into the barn.

Niall grabbed her arm and pulled her back towards him. Before he realized what was happening, he'd pulled her tight against him and covered her mouth with his. She stood ramrod straight, her arms at her sides. He gentled the kiss but not the pressure. Her hands moved slowly up his arms, rested on his shoulders, and crept up to encircle his neck. The kiss deepened. He was vaguely aware this was not the kiss of an experienced woman, but of someone who had little, if any, experience. He pushed the thought out of his mind.

Niall needed more. His tongue moved across her sealed lips, once, twice, coaxing them to open. Her involuntary sigh achieved what he wanted, and when his tongue began to explore her mouth, Kate froze and started to push at his shoulders. His sanity returned abruptly and he dropped his hands to his sides. They stood staring at each other for a few seconds before his hand tightened on Misty's reins, then he turned his back to Kate and strode out of the barn.

******

86

Kate didn't pretend the kiss wasn't what she wanted. Her mind had been occupied for several days with trying to regain her memory, teaching Beth, and thinking of Niall. Even when working with Beth, Kate's mind was on Niall. As much as she tried to push the thought aside, it now seemed hopeless to rid him from her thoughts.

The ring on her finger was a constant reminder that someone might be waiting for her, but every instinct she had told her there was no husband, no children, no one to stop her from wanting Niall. Not knowing for certain was torture. Not that he was interested in her. She'd heard the talk about his Friday nights with Gloria, as well as his desire to wed Mrs. Jocelyn van Deelin. Kate had met her at church, and agreed with the descriptions Alicia and others used when they thought no one was around. They'd referred to her as cold and condescending. The woman was committed to few things from what the ladies had said, but those included enlarging her social circle, gaining more wealth, and marrying Niall.

The MacLarens did not have extreme wealth, but Niall had built the ranch into one of the most secure in the region. It was said that business matters came as naturally to him as ranching. There was even talk that if Niall ever wanted to, he could run for office. Kate knew he scoffed at those comments from the conversations around the supper table, but he was sincere about being involved in structuring the future of Fire Mountain, as well as the Arizona territory. Marrying Jocelyn to gain her connections and enlarge his already expanding operation would provide all the power he needed to be sure his was a serious voice in decisions about the territory. That last thought brought Kate back to the reality of her situation. He had land, money, political connections, and planned to expand all three through an advantageous marriage. She was an utter fool to spend even a little time wishing for something she could never have. Niall was as far out of her reach as her memory.

Chapter Eleven

"Two more robberies this week. Thief took jewelry from the Delvecchio place and the same, plus cash, from the Castalan ranch." Sheriff Rawlins spoke to a small group of men outside the Desert Dove the following week. He knew all of them well and trusted each implicitly. "No one knows for sure when everything was taken, but we do know that both families attended a get-together on Saturday at your place, Niall."

"Beth's birthday," Niall replied. He considered the sheriff's words for a minute. "So if I am reading you right, Sheriff, this could be the first lead you have into the thefts."

"You're reading me right, Niall," the sheriff answered as the others looked on in confusion. "I spoke again with those who had items stolen. All had attended some type of shindig not long before they found things were missing. Each gathering was common knowledge, not short-notice, and included entire families."

"Meaning everyone was gone from the home, correct, Sheriff?" Sam asked.

"That's right. It seems to me someone could use this information to plan the thefts. Remember, nothing's been damaged, no one hurt, and darned little taken, given the amount of jewelry left behind." That was the part that frustrated the sheriff the most. Why were some pieces taken and not others? Small, seemingly insignificant, jewelry had been stolen. More valuable pieces had been left behind. There was a definite pattern, but damn if he could figure it out.

"Well," Doc Minton started, looking at Hen Wright who owned the hotel and mercantile in Fire Mountain, "sounds to me like it's a good time for you to have that anniversary celebration you've been considering, Hen. You'll just need to be selective in who you invite."

"What the hell are you talking about?" Hen had no idea what Doc was suggesting until he saw eyes light up around him. "Of course. A small celebration may just draw them out. The ranchers I'd invite would have enough help to protect their property, and I'd invite townspeople whose homes could be watched. What do you say, Sheriff?"

Rawlins turned to his new deputy. "What are your thoughts, Sam?"

Sam hadn't been in Fire Mountain long, but he'd gained considerable experience as a deputy in other growing towns. He was also thoughtful, and not prone to jump into action before considering several options. "Could work. Set the date a week out, so the thief has time to plan, and we have time to set up men at each place. Niall, your brother anywhere near?" Sam asked.

"Both Drew and Will are here. You know that Sam."

"No, I mean Jamie. Still with the Marshals Service, isn't he? It'd be good to have him with us on this."

Jamie¬¬¬¬¬¬¬¬¬--Niall hadn't heard from him in a long time, but Jamie did keep in touch with their aunt. If he didn't, Alicia would send men out to find him, and Jamie knew it.

"You know Jamie?"

"Worked with him on a couple of cases over the last few years, in Phoenix and New Mexico. Good man. If he's close and available, he'd be a big help." Sam answered back.

"Don't know where he is. Could do some checking, if you think we need him." Niall didn't want to reach out to Jamie. Niall needed him to come back on his own, not because he felt obligated.

"Last I heard he was in Tucson, working some kidnappings. He's real good at it, too. Has a reputation for finding people and bringing them home." Sam said the last with purpose, and the meaning was not lost on Niall. "I'll put the request out to him if it's okay with you." Niall nodded. Anyone else reaching out to Jamie would be better than him.

"What about the big dance this weekend? Too late to make it part of the plan, but people ought to be made aware, don't you think, Sheriff?" Jerrod Minton, Doc's oldest son, had listened to the plans being made around him without commenting, which was unusual. He was the most successful lawyer in town, and could be counted on for a well-thought-out opinion on just about everything. He was also head of the town council, and his clients included most of the ranchers in the area, including the MacLaren's.

"Sam and I will put the word out to the ranchers and townsfolk. Let everyone know to lock up anything valuable if they go to the dance. It's bound to get to those doing the thieving, maybe make them think better of it and move on." Rawlins paused a minute. "We could have Atkinson open up the bank to let people use his vault that night. Let the robbers know that nothing of value will be available for the taking. We all agreed?"

The sheriff's approach had merit, thought Niall. Take the incentive away for the dance, but leave it in plain sight for Hen's get together.

"Sounds good to me, Sheriff." Doc voiced the thoughts of all the men as everyone disbursed, with Niall heading towards the Desert Dove.

******

Niall didn't understand the thoughts rolling through him or the unease he felt. Here he was at Gloria's place, in her room, watching her slip the gown from her shoulders, and all he could think about was riding back to the ranch. Ever since that kiss at Beth's party, he'd been calling himself every type of fool, while reminding himself that Kate was married and off limits. But their kiss had changed things somehow.

Ever since that chance meeting in Phoenix, a meeting Kate didn't remember, he'd wanted to kiss her, and more. His instincts told him it would be good between them, but nothing had quite prepared him for their kiss or her innocence. Maybe she hadn't been married long, maybe it had been a forced marriage, maybe her husband was an inexperienced or thoughtless lover, or maybe he was deceiving himself.

"Niall? You look a million miles away. Anything wrong? Do you want to talk?" Gloria sounded more concerned than hurt or irritated. Anyone else would be upset by his lack of attention, but Gloria knew him too well.

"Sorry Gloria, but I don't feel like talking. Probably shouldn't have even come here tonight. I think I'll ride back to the ranch and turn in. It's been a long week, and next week will be the same."

"What are you going to do about her, Niall?"

"Jocelyn? You know my plans. I've never kept them a secret from you."

Fact was they both knew that Gloria cared deeply for Niall, had for years, but she'd never use it against him, or expect anything more than what he already gave. She'd made her choices years ago, and blamed no one but herself for her lonely life. Unlike some in her position, she owned her business, made good money, and saved a great deal of it. Jerrod Minton was her attorney and Pat Atkinson her banker. Between the three of them, decisions had been made that were now setting her up to sell the business in a few years and retire to some place far away, where no one would know her, and she could start over. Maybe find someone like Niall—a man she could love, and who would love her.

"No, Niall, I mean your houseguest, Kate. When are you going to figure out that you have feelings for her, and not the brotherly type?" Sometimes Niall could be just downright dense.

"I don't know what the hell you're talking about. Kate means nothing to me other than as a governess to Beth. When she regains her memory, she'll be out

93

of here on the next stage, heading back to her husband, or whatever life she has waiting for her. No, I haven't the least interest in anyone or anything that will alter my plans with Jocelyn."

He was working himself up, which was unusual, unless he had strong feelings for her and refused to accept them. Gloria pondered this as she refastened the last button on her gown and fussed with her hair.

"Well, it's best you get back to the ranch and get your sleep. When do you and Jocelyn plan to announce your betrothal? It seems to me that most everyone expects it anytime now. Maybe at the dance tomorrow would be good. Everyone will be there."

Niall let out a slow breath before answering. "I haven't asked her yet. It's something we seem to accept is coming and will work well financially for both of us. Right now, I need to get Beth accustomed to her. Like you've mentioned several times," his eyes narrowed at Gloria, "Jocelyn doesn't take well to children, and Beth has made it clear she wants no part of Jocelyn. At some point, Beth will have to accept it. I don't know what the timing is, Gloria, and I don't want to think about it tonight." With that, Niall placed a soft kiss on Gloria's cheek and left without a backward glance.

******

The house was finally quiet. It was midnight. Beth had gone to bed hours ago, and Alicia not long afterwards. Drew and Will had called it a night, but Kate just couldn't settle down enough to sleep. She lay in bed for a couple of hours, then gave up, put on her wrapper, and walked down the stairs to check out the library in Niall's office, which she did many nights. Niall, and Drew, as well as their uncle before them, were avid readers, and the selection was immense for a private home.

Kate opened the door and peeked in, but the room was still. She walked to a table next to the bookshelves and lit the oil lamp. She found something promising that might make her sleepy, sat down on the sofa, and opened the book. She was settling into the story when she caught movement by the desk. The chair Niall used was large and high-backed. Tonight it was positioned facing the windows behind the desk, which provided an excellent view of the barn and bunkhouse, and effectively hid them from anyone entering the darkened room.

A figure emerged from the chair and turned to face Kate. He held a drink in one hand. Even though Kate knew instinctively who it was, she gasped at his sudden appearance.

"Sneaking around my office are you?" Niall's voice was thick and his words slurred. "Do you snoop often when I'm away from the ranch?" His accusatory tone hurt, but Kate held his gaze as she closed the book and stood with her hands clasped in front of her.

"I don't sneak, and I don't snoop, Mr. MacLaren. Maybe that's what you'd do in my place, but I have no interest or desire to learn more about you. I've already learned enough about your rude, condescending nature. My focus is learning more about me. Reading sometimes triggers memories, and I'll try whatever I must to regain my life." Kate was working up to being angry. Her clear blue eyes sparked as her words cut through the quiet room. Her blonde hair was down, twisted into one long braid, and she wore nothing but a sheer nightdress and wrapper. She was the most beautiful woman Niall had ever seen.

Camille had been pretty, very pretty, with long, chestnut brown hair and soft brown eyes. Her eyes were what had drawn Niall to her years ago, big, round, and trusting. She was taller than Kate, about five feet eight inches, which fit his six foot two frame well. She was slim, but well-endowed, which Niall had appreciated. Camille was quiet by nature and raised her voice on very rare occasions, which suited Niall, as he disliked women who were always voicing their opinions and trying to excel at men's work. And he'd loved her.

So why did he have feelings for someone who was Camille's opposite? Someone who let her opinion be known, rode and handled a gun like a man, looked you straight in the eye without flinching, was well educated, short, at around five feet four inches, with a slender frame, and striking blonde hair? Hair that shown like the sun. Hair that made him want to walk up to her, unfurl her braid, and run his hands through it in long, slow strokes. Hair that he suspected was soft to the touch, and would slide over him as they made love. That last thought had him staring down at his whiskey. He downed it in one swallow and slammed the glass down on the desk.

He strolled right up to Kate, in her space, glaring down at her with a scowl and troubled eyes. "Just make sure books are all you're looking at in this place. If I catch you doing anything else, you'll be out of here as fast as you arrived, with no regrets on my part." The only reaction he saw was slight tearing, which could have been the light reflecting in her eyes, or the effects of the whiskey on his, but she stood her ground and didn't flinch when he brushed by her and out the office door.

She could hear his footsteps, heavy on the stairs. His tirade had jarred her, but she was determined he wouldn't see how it affected her. It was all the worse as her feelings for him were so strong. She didn't know if she felt this way about her husband, assuming she had one, but every time she was around Niall she was nervous, excited, and confused. It was unsettling. Why did he dislike her so? Didn't he know that if she had anywhere else to go, she would? She would miss Beth, Alicia, and the twins, more than she cared to think about, but she now knew her time here was short, even if she never did regain her memory. She would start to make inquiries about moving into town, and finding another position. There must be another family who could use her services. At this point, she would clean hotel rooms, work in the mercantile, do just about anything to get away from Niall and his constant scolding.

Tomorrow night was the dance. Alicia insisted she go with the family and ranch hands. They'd been busy making dresses for the three females, plus baking bread, pies, and cookies, as Alicia said everyone for miles would be coming. The dance would be the perfect place to make discreet inquiries and put her own plans in motion.

Chapter Twelve

Morning arrived too soon, and with it the final preparations for the party. Kate hadn't slept well. She tossed and turned all night, trying to forget the conversation with Niall, and his malicious behavior.

Alicia had everyone helping to load the wagon by the time Kate came down stairs. All but two or three of the ranch hands would attend the dance. Gus had always stayed behind before, but this year he'd decided to tag along, designating a couple of the other hands to take his place at home.

They finished loading the wagon about one o'clock, and started for town. Alicia, as was her custom, volunteered to help setup, which meant Kate had also volunteered. This suited her fine, as it would give her a start at inquiring about other positions. She wasn't sure how she'd go about it without Alicia finding out, but the tension between her and Niall, after the confrontation in the library last night, had further confirmed that her decision was the right one.

******

The dance was going strong by eight o'clock. Food was still plentiful, punch was flowing, and the band was drawing many to take advantage of the big dance platform the men had erected. Kate danced with so many men she had to beg off a couple of times. There was an abundance of men, which left little time for any single woman to rest.

Sam Browning had come by several times for a dance, which pleased her immensely. He was a good dancer and kept the conversation going with stories and jokes that made her laugh. It was so different from being around Niall, who never missed a chance to let her how little she meant to him.

Niall, of course, brought Jocelyn van Deelin, and had spared little time for anyone else, except short conversations with the family and other ranchers. Jocelyn clung to him the entire night, not letting him get more than a few feet away. He didn't seem to notice that anyone else existed––especially not Kate.

"Kate, would you care to dance?" Niall stood at her elbow, touching it lightly in a gesture to escort her to the floor. Her surprise must have been obvious. "I promise I won't bite," Niall said with a slight smile.

Biting isn't what concerns me, she thought, but nodded to Niall. "Yes, a dance would be nice if you promise not to accuse me of anything.'

Niall winced. He'd been a real bastard to her since she'd arrived, and he well knew it. He'd had no intention of asking Kate to dance tonight. He'd planned to stay as far away from her as possible, and to be the perfect partner to Jocelyn. But watching the constant stream of men dancing with her, holding her, getting too close to her, was pushing him to the edge. His whiskey glass had been refilled several times as he watched her dance, smile, and laugh with everyone but him. He shouldn't feel this way. There were so many things he didn't know about her, plus, there was a very real chance she was married.

And there was Jocelyn. Niall had decided he'd take Jocelyn to her place after the dance and ask her to marry him. That would put Kate far out of his mind and his reach.

But here he was walking Kate onto the dance floor, and taking her in his arms. She looked right, felt right, and smelled right. He wanted her with an intensity he'd never felt for any woman before, not even Camille. It was sobering, but it was the truth. He'd made it a point to never get involved with married women, preferring his relationship with Gloria. The only innocent he'd ever been with was his bride, Camille. He needed to stop this insanity before he crossed the line, and made everyone's life more complicated.

"You're a good dancer, Mr. MacLaren." His movements were fluid as he led her around the floor to a slow tune.

"I would prefer it if you'd call me Niall. After all, I can't very well call you by your married name, since we don't know it."

Kate had to laugh at the logical statement. "All right, Niall then. Did your mother teach you to dance?"

He stared down at her for a bit before answering. "Yes. She'd learned when she was young, and was determined to see her boys grow up with civilized skills. After she died, and we moved to the ranch, Aunt Alicia took up the job with a vengeance. I can be civilized when the occasion calls for it, Kate."

Her name rolling from his lips sent a chill through her. It was only a name, but coming from Niall, it seemed so much more. She shut her eyes to clear her head and focus on his comment. She had no doubt he could be very civilized and charming. According to town gossip, every unattached woman under thirty-five was in mourning that he seemed to have settled on Jocelyn. Kate tried not to care, but there was an ache in the area of her heart when she thought of the two of them together. Yes, leaving the ranch would be the best for all of them.

They were quiet for the rest of the dance. He pulled her closer and lowered his head to her hair. It was soft and still smelled of sunshine, even though the sun had vanished hours ago. His hand rubbed slow circles low on her back, and she rested her head on his chest. Niall slowed their pace. The music stopped. He continued to hold her, longer than necessary, before she raised her head and stared into his intense green eyes.

The truth hit Kate hard and fast. She was in love with this man and there was no hope for it.

It took all his will power not to lower his head for the kiss he knew they both wanted. He recognized desire when he saw it, and what he saw in Kate's eyes mirrored his own—but not here, not ever. Niall released Kate, walked her to her seat, made a slight bow, and headed back to Jocelyn.

"Do you mind telling me what that was about?" Jocelyn was irritated at the obvious display on the dance floor.

"I don't know what you're asking, Jocelyn. She is a guest in my home, and Beth's governess. It was

proper to ask her for a dance, and that's all it was."
He hated being questioned about his relationships
and would not be drawn into a discussion about
Kate, especially with Jocelyn.

Jocelyn scowled at him, but decided it wasn't
worth pursuing. They were seeing each other for
reasons beyond a romantic involvement, and if he
wanted one, two, or three whores on the side, what
did it matter to her? All she would ask of him, if they
married, was that he keep his liaisons discreet.

Niall's eyes drifted back to the dance floor and
landed on Kate, again in the arms of Sam Browning.
He guessed this was their third or fourth dance and
his gut twisted. He excused himself and moved to
the bar for one more drink to calm his growing
anger, before he did something stupid that he'd
regret.

"Do you want to tell me what that was about?"
Gus was at his side, staring straight at Kate, the
same as Niall. The long-time ranch foreman didn't
miss much when it came to the MacLaren boys.

"Hell, Gus, you, too?" Niall poured a whiskey
and downed it in one swallow.

"She's a beauty, no doubt about that, but
trouble. Big time trouble if you ask me."

"Well no one is asking you. Besides, you know
as well as I do that I'll be asking Jocelyn to marry
me soon." Niall started to grab the bottle for one
more shot, but Gus's hand clamped on his arm
before he could pour.

"Trust me, you don't want another drink. Go get
Jocelyn and walk her home. Ask what you came
here to ask her, then ride home and sleep it off. If

103

marrying the van Deelin woman is what you want, then it's time to move on it and let any feelings for Kate go."

Niall just stared at Gus. Of course that's what he wanted. It's what he'd wanted for some time now. Gus was right. Time to move on it.

Chapter Thirteen

Kate helped gather Beth and, along with Alicia, boarded the wagon for the ride home. Funny how she called it home, even as she knew her time there was short. Her inquiries regarding open positions had proven fruitful. Two families were seeking live-in help for their children. Both were ranchers who lived miles from town and the regular school. One had two children and the other had three. She needed to learn more about each, but before she did anything further, she needed to determine if they were close friends of the MacLaren's. They must know each other, but she didn't want to pit one family against the other, even though she knew that Niall would be glad she was leaving.

The dance with Niall had been eye opening, at least for her. The attraction she felt for him was too strong, and she was afraid––afraid love for him would cloud her reason. She couldn't afford to do anything stupid.

Once Beth was settled in bed, Kate built a fire in her room. She dressed in a lightweight gown, removed the pins from her hair, and brushed it for several minutes before finishing with a braid. She walked to the bed, pulled back the covers, and snuggled beneath them before opening a book, hoping to rest her mind and find sleep. But it wouldn't come. Kate turned the lamp off and burrowed deeper under the blankets.

Sometime later, she was still in the same position, and wide awake. She knew Niall had left the dance with Jocelyn about the same time their own wagon had started for the ranch. She'd been home over two hours and still had heard no sounds indicating Niall had returned. Perhaps Alicia's guess was right, and he had asked Jocelyn to marry him. The pain in her heart was immediate and intense. How had she let this happen? She closed her eyes and willed her brain to turn off, but all she could see was Niall with Jocelyn, holding her, smiling into her eyes when she said yes to his request to marry, kissing her. Niall with Jocelyn, and not with her.

She heard a door open, then close, and footsteps coming up the steps. Niall walked past her room and hesitated for a minute. Kate's heart stopped, and she held her breath. Would he knock, ask to see her? No. It was just a short pause, a few seconds, before he walked on to his own room and closed the door. Her heart sank.

Kate snuggled deeper into the soft bed and closed her eyes. She tried to sleep—willed herself to sleep—but the events of the night wouldn't be stilled. Impatient with herself, Kate gave up, threw off the covers, and walked to the fireplace. She added a couple more logs and stoked the fire, stood, watching as the flames rose, bathing the room in a warm glow. She heard her doorknob turn, and the door open. Niall stood inside her room in bare feet, dressed only in his dress pants.

His skin was darkened from the summer months of working without a shirt. His body was muscled from the heavy work a ranch required. His dark hair was tousled as if he, too, had been lying awake in bed, unable to sleep. His arms hung limp at his sides. His expressive green eyes bored into hers as she turned to face him.

Does she know that with the fire behind her, I can see right through that nightdress? It was as if she had nothing on. Even as he advanced toward her, he knew he shouldn't have come. This was wrong in so many ways. But his body had a mind of its own and he was unable to deny it.

He'd taken Jocelyn home, but after an hour Niall still hadn't been able to work up the will to ask her to marry him. The words wouldn't form in his mouth. She'd prattled on about the dance, the boring townspeople, the utter lack of significant social functions, and how she wondered why so many families kept their children at home instead of sending them to boarding schools, as was the custom back east. The last remark finally got his attention. He had no intention of sending his daughter away, and needed to get the issue settled before asking Jocelyn to marry him. He'd said his goodbyes and ridden back to the ranch, thinking about Kate the entire time. He thought of the way her eyes sparkled when she laughed, her patience teaching Beth, the kindness she'd shown Alicia, and her willingness to pitch in, as if she were a real part of the family. He couldn't get the images of her at the dance out of his mind—images of her laughing, moving without effort around the dance floor, relaxed and confident as she spoke with the other men. He should've been the one dancing with her all night. He wanted Kate to look at him and laugh the way she did with the other men. He wanted...

Now he was in her room, half dressed, and wanting nothing more than to pick her up and take her to bed. He advanced slowly, waiting for her to make a sound, to tell him to stop, but she just watched him advance.

"I shouldn't be here," Niall whispered. "You belong to someone else."

Kate said nothing, just continued to stare into those dark pools of emerald green. Niall stopped a couple of feet away.

"We don't have a future." His throat worked as the words came out. He wanted, needed, Kate to understand that the pull between them, if they acted on it, wouldn't change his plans. He advanced until she was only inches away. "Tonight won't change anything," he rasped, the words barely discernible. "We can only have this one night."

Still, Kate stood without speaking. Nothing would come. She wanted him to be here, wanted him to touch her. She knew what Niall said was true, *only one night*, but her mind could not coerce the words from her mouth, the words that would stop him. Kate stood her ground, a small nod indicating she had heard him.

Niall took a deep, ragged breath before bringing a hand up to caress her face, cup her cheek. Kate closed her eyes and leaned into his warm palm. Niall then did what he'd wanted to do for weeks. He reached behind her, pulled the braid forward, and unwrapped it, taking his time. He slid his right hand to encircle the back of her neck and captured the soft, inviting locks that shone in the firelight. He ran the strands through his fingers as if he had all night, repeating the process over and over, as he'd done in his fantasies.

Kate's head fell back and a moan escaped her lips. Taking his time, Niall pulled her to him and captured her mouth for a long kiss, marveling at her response. She felt herself melt into him. This time her lips opened willingly.

Niall became more demanding, eager to take what he'd wanted for weeks. His left hand pressed against her back to draw her flush against him. He could feel her breasts, soft and compliant against his chest, and at that moment he knew he wouldn't turn back—-not unless she pushed him away.

Kate could feel Niall's arousal through her gown. She'd never felt this before; she knew it instantly. This feeling was something that couldn't be suppressed, even with a loss of memory. It was too strong. Her arms were around his neck but she had no idea how they'd gotten there. All she knew was that she didn't want him to break the kiss or the warmth of contact between her body and his. She was vaguely aware of his left hand leaving her back, moving over her stomach to cup her right breast, creating a trail of heat. He caressed it gently, enjoying the fullness. Her knees gave way and he caught her, lifted her in his arms, and carried her to the bed.

Niall set her down and stared into her passion filled eyes. "Tell me to stop, Kate. Tell me to go back to my room, that you don't want this." Niall was almost pleading for a way out.

Kate's eyes met his, sure and steady. "I do want this, Niall. I want you."

The little will power he had left snapped. He grabbed the hem of her gown, pulled it up and over her head, and let it drop in a pool by the bed. She wore nothing underneath. Niall could barely breathe. God help him, she was perfect. "Ah Kate, you are so very beautiful."

She edged closer to him and grazed his chest with her fingers. Her touch was gentle, tentative. She brought her other hand up and pressed both flat onto his broad chest to cover the dark, course hair. She took her time running her hands across it, feeling the difference between her and Niall. He groaned, captured her hands to kiss each finger, and pushed her back onto the bed.

Kate watched him undress. He climbed onto the bed, stretching out so they lay face to face, body to body. He kissed her. Soft kisses that wandered over her lips, her cheeks, down her neck and chest, and lingered on her breasts, his tongue teasing. Kate moaned in pleasure and pushed herself against him. He took his time, moving to the other breast and repeating the process. His right hand made circles on her stomach then moved lower.

"Open for me, Kate." It was all the invitation she needed. Kate would have done anything for him at that moment. She gasped as his ministrations created a heat that took her by surprise.

"Niall. Please..." Kate pleaded, her voice so low he barcly heard as he kept up the plcasurable torture.

"Have you never felt like this, Kate?"

Kate shook her head in slow movements from side to side as a soft moan escaped her lips. She had no idea what was happening, but the heat was building, the sensations growing. Her back arched. Release came as a surprise, startling his name from her lips.

The vibrations continued to move through her then subsided gradually. Kate became aware of Niall moving over her and positioning himself above her. Reality hit hard as Kate realized what he was doing. "Niall, wait. I need time. I'm not ready."

Misinterpreting her meaning he whispered into her ear, "Ah, Kate, you couldn't be more ready for me. But, if you want me to stop, say so now, and I will," Niall rasped, finding it hard to maintain control.

Kate's breathing had slowed and her fogged mind began to clear. No, she didn't want Niall to stop. She wanted this man and this night. Their eyes met and locked. "I want you, Niall. I want this."

Niall took a steadying breath as he eased into her with one sure stroke. It happened so fast he almost missed the barrier he had no idea was there. Kate gasped. Her eyes squeezed shut. *What the hell*, thought Niall?

He was stunned by the revelation that Kate had been a virgin. He stilled, waiting for Kate to adjust to him and relax.

"Kate?" Niall asked. She opened her eyes to see concern etched on his face.

"Don't stop, Niall. Please don't stop," she pleaded when she realized what he was asking. His smile was filled with tenderness as he accepted her answer.

Her muscles eased and he started to move in and out in a gentle rhythm. Kate found she had begun to match his strokes.

Niall had never experienced anything this intense with a woman. She gave back everything he was giving her. It was natural, not forced––and it was her first time.

Kate felt the same warmth as before, only this was more powerful. Niall continued to move with her, increasing his pace until his neck muscles were taut and his body strained. Kate's release the second time was even more intense. She chanted his name, over and over. Moments later Niall followed her to his own release.

******

Niall pushed off Kate, rolled to his back, and placed his arm across his eyes, his emotions raging. This night, with Kate, was more passionate than anything he'd ever felt. He was more fulfilled than at any time before, but also more confused. There was no future with this woman. Even with what they'd learned tonight, there was still good reason to believe she belonged to someone else, and if his future unfolded as expected, he would marry another. No matter how he felt about Kate, no matter how much he wanted her, he couldn't let his emotions rule his mind.

"Kate?" Niall didn't turn to her.

"Don't say it, Niall. Please don't say it." Kate lay beside him, watching the internal struggle play across his face, all the while knowing she would lose. At least now she knew for certain she'd been a virgin, possibly never been married. Before tonight, she'd longed to have a chance with Niall. Now she knew the likelihood of her being married to someone else was slim, but he was lost to her anyway. He'd made it clear when he stepped across her threshold that there was no future for them. They had only this one time of shared pleasure. She had accepted it, and now she would have to live with her decision.

Niall rolled off the bed and began to dress, his movements slow, his guilt immense. He was the worst kind of bastard, he knew it, but still, he was determined to move forward with Jocelyn.

"I know you must hate me, Kate," his words were clear but the defeat in his voice pierced her heart.

"No, Niall, I don't hate you. I wanted this, with you. How could I hate you?" Kate struggled to control the tears that threatened.

"But you were a virgin. How could that be?"

"I don't know, but does it matter? Perhaps my husband died before our wedding night. Perhaps mine is a marriage of convenience or the ring was given to me as a gift. It doesn't change the fact that someone may still be waiting for me." The sadness Niall heard in her words nearly broke him.

The best thing he could do was end this, now. It was Sunday. He'd invite Jocelyn to dinner and ask her to marry him with everyone present, put a stop to this insanity, and build a final barrier between him and Kate.

"Please try to understand, Kate. I won't love again. I gave everything I had to Camille. Now I

113

must do what's best for Beth, and the rest of my family. There's nothing left to give to you. I'm going to ask Jocelyn to marry me." Niall tried to see Kate's face, but she turned away.

"I understand, Niall. We both know my future is uncertain. You and your family have done so much, and I'm truly grateful. But, you're right. You don't love me, and never will. I don't belong to you and you don't belong to me." She was thankful the fire had died down. Tears rolled down her face, but Niall couldn't see them in the darkened room.

Niall reached for the doorknob but turned to look back at Kate, huddled in bed with the covers pulled around her. "I'm so sorry, Kate." He closed the door quietly, leaving her alone.

Several minutes passed before Kate was able to summon her strength and edge her way off the bed. That's when she noticed the blood. Oh God, what now? She had to clean it before Alicia saw it and discovered what had happened. But tonight she was too exhausted and sick. Kate fell back into bed, falling asleep just as the sun began to rise.

Chapter Fourteen

"Niall, you and Beth go on to church without me. Kate's not well, and she doesn't look good. She's not running a fever, but I don't want to leave her alone." Alicia usually didn't worry much over a sick adult, but Niall could see she was concerned about Kate.

He wondered if he he'd hurt her last night. "All right, Aunt Alicia. I had planned to bring Jocelyn to the ranch for dinner. Should I put it off for another time?" Now that he'd made his decision, Niall wanted to move forward.

"No, dinner would be fine. I'm sure Kate will be feeling better by then. We'll see you all this afternoon. Have a good time, Beth."

"Do we have to bring that lady over for dinner, Papa?" Beth's question wasn't unexpected. She didn't like Jocelyn. Alicia had once said children were excellent judges of character, but he wasn't marrying Jocelyn for her character. He was marrying her for her connections and land, pure and simple.

"Yes, Beth, we do if she accepts my invitation. What is it you don't like about Mrs. van Deelin anyway? Isn't she always nice to you?"

"Uh-uh," she shook her head vigorously. "She doesn't like me, I can tell. She doesn't treat me like Kate does. Kate is nice and funny and gives me hugs. Why can't you like Kate instead, Papa? She loves the ranch and I love her. I don't want Mrs. van Deelin at the ranch." Beth fell silent, but her words rolled over and over in Niall's mind.

******

"Oh, what a stunning dinner setting, Mrs. MacLaren. Everything looks just wonderful," Jocelyn gushed as she walked into the dining room. She'd been eager to accept Niall's invitation, even while she knew Beth didn't want her to come. Jocelyn hoped he'd made the decision to ask her to marry and join their influence. She was certain that, together, they'd have the power to move into the highest political circles of Arizona, ultimately occupying the Governor's seat. She knew everyone thought she aspired to a higher life in the east, but what she craved was being the first lady of the territory, with all the privileges the title included. Such a sweet deal for both of them. And, as soon as they were married, she'd find a way to move Alicia to town and Beth to a boarding school. She had no intention of sharing the same house with the older, meddling woman and Niall's disruptive daughter. Unless of course, she and her husband were settled in a mansion at the capital.

"Why, thank you, Jocelyn. My late husband, Stuart, gave me the set. We use it for Sunday dinners and special occasions. Well, if you will excuse me, I'd like to check on Kate to see if she'll join us. Niall, will you let Drew and Will know everything is ready?"

Alicia treaded up the stairs, knowing there was something wrong with Kate, perhaps between Kate and Niall, but she couldn't imagine what it could be since he paid so little attention to her. Then again, he sure did seem to take notice of her last night at the dance. Today, however, Kate seemed miserable, but not due to sickness. Alicia didn't know what to make of it.

"I'm sorry, Alicia, but I don't feel well enough to go down stairs. Please allow me to take my meal up here after everyone has left. I don't want to ruin dinner." Kate wasn't dressed and looked so distressed that Alicia didn't push her.

"Of course, Kate. I'll let Niall and Jocelyn know you aren't feeling well. Get some sleep and I'll check on you later."

Alicia informed Niall of Kate's decision. He turned abruptly and took the steps two at a time, then pounded down the hall to Kate's room and threw open the door. He came to a dead stop at the sight of her. She was pale, her normally clear blue eyes a washed out grey. It appeared she hadn't been able to sleep after he'd left her room. He hadn't slept either. Worst of all, she grabbed the blankets tightly around her, moved back to the headboard with her knees up against her chest, and held her hands up to ward him off, as if he were planning to harm her.

"Kate, what is it? Did I hurt you last night?" Niall's concern was evident.

"No, Niall, you didn't hurt me." *Not physically, anyway.* "I'm tired and have no desire to visit with your guest right now." Kate had a hard time understanding why he'd brought Jocelyn to the ranch so soon after their night together. Didn't he realize how much pain it would cause Kate to sit through dinner with the woman who would be his wife? Did he have no feelings for her whatsoever?

"Kate, I thought we agreed last night to move on with our plans. I'll be asking Jocelyn to marry me. I believe it's best if I do it today, with everyone present, including you, unless you've changed your mind and wish to make this more difficult for both of us." Niall's words were direct but not harsh. She understood his desire to put behind them what had happened last night. She just wasn't sure she could witness it.

"No," Kate said. She tried to rally and steady her voice, but it came out flat. "No, Niall. I know there's no future for us. You made it very clear."

His gut twisted. "Life doesn't always work out the way we want, Kate." Niall was desperate to keep his emotions in check and not let her get to him. He'd push his feelings for Kate aside and marry Jocelyn. "I'll never be able to love you the way you deserve and you have a life somewhere we know nothing about." He had no wish to hurt Kate, but he had to sever any remaining feelings they might have for each other. "I've come to take you downstairs to dinner. I'm asking you not to make this harder on either of us than it already is." His green eyes had turned an intense, dark emerald and bored directly into hers. He wasn't going to budge. She could see the determination on his face.

"All right," she conceded, resigned to a future without him in it. She knew he was right. The fact remained she could be married, although her heart told her it wasn't true. She'd make a quick appearance, watch him propose to another, excuse herself, and come back to her room to begin packing her few possessions. She would ask to be taken into town tonight. "I'll dress and be down shortly."

Niall nodded and closed the door. He no longer felt enthusiasm for the future he'd planned before he met Kate. As he descended the stairs he wondered, for at least the twentieth time that day, if he was making the biggest mistake of his life.

******

It was a somber meal, not like the usual Sunday dinners with Drew and Will cracking jokes, Beth laughing, and Kate enjoying every minute of it. No, this was nothing like the other family meals. Kate didn't want to be here. She couldn't look at either Niall or Jocelyn, and had no desire to join the conversations Alicia tried to initiate. Kate moved the food around her plate but had no appetite. It wasn't a lie when she'd told Alicia and Niall she felt sick, but it was more a sickness of the heart than anything else. She couldn't focus on the people at the table, or the food, when her thoughts were so jumbled. It didn't help that Niall stared at her much of the meal, glancing away only on those few occasions when she did raise her head.

Alicia pushed back her chair to stand. "Let me clear these plates and I'll get dessert."

Niall's words stopped her. "Wait a minute please, Aunt Alicia. I have something to say." He stood and looked at those around the table. "As you all know, Jocelyn and I have been seeing each other for a few months and have found we have much in common." Niall paused to gaze around the table at the most important people in his life. The expressions on the faces of his family members didn't encourage him. Drew shook his head in disgust. Will leaned back in his chair, and wouldn't meet his eyes. Alicia sat in stoic silence, lips thin, with no hint of a smile or her normal warmth.

He turned to Jocelyn. The look in her eyes showed smug confidence, almost arrogance, as she sensed she was about to snatch a prize. It unsettled him. Was this what he wanted? To spend a life with this woman? Niall shifted his gaze to Kate and took a deep breath.

"Hey, anyone around?" Niall would know that voice anywhere.

"Jamie!" Several voices said at once. Drew and Will jumped up before Niall could say anything further, and moved toward the man standing at the entrance to the dining room.

"Hey, brother, it's great to see you." Drew slapped Jamie on the back at the same time Will offered his hand to his older brother and pulled him into a hug.

Niall stood off to the side, waiting for the twins to finish their hellos, before also offering his hand. "Jamie, welcome home."

Jamie accepted Niall's hand and shook it before walking up to his waiting aunt and giving her a bear hug.

"Jamie, what a wonderful surprise. It's so good to see you."

"It's good to see you, too, Aunt Alicia." Jamie had missed his aunt, and regretted that his chosen profession always kept him away so long.

"Uncle Jamie!" Beth jumped into his arms as he bent to grab her and swing her around.

"Beth, you've grown a foot since the last time I was here. How are you, peanut?" *How long have I been gone, anyway?* Jamie thought. "Why, I believe you've grown two-feet since the last time I was home."

"I'm seven, and Aunt Alicia and Miss Kate make me wear dresses all the time now." This last was said with revulsion and a slight pout.

"Well, you're real pretty, Beth, and very grown up." Jamie's words had the desired effect as Beth beamed up at him and moved back next to her father. "And who is this Miss Kate?" His eyes scanned the table and lit on a pale blonde who was trying to make herself invisible on the other side of the table.

Alicia spoke up first. "Jamie, meet Kate, Beth's governess. Kate, this is the fourth brother, Jamie. He has a habit of popping in at the most unexpected times." Jamie walked around the table and gazed down at Kate, offering his hand.

"Pleased to meet you Miss..." Jamie started.

"Umm, it's Kate...just Kate." The words were whispered as she took his hand.

Another man suddenly appeared in the doorway.

"My God, is that who I think it is?" Niall walked up to the man and offered his hand. "Trent Garner, I haven't seen you in these parts in, what, a couple of years?"

At the mention of his name, Kate's head snapped around. She stared directly at the stranger. But he wasn't a stranger. He was the exact image of the man she'd seen in her visions, and his name ignited something in her mind, but she couldn't settle on what it was.

"Niall." Garner took the offered hand and shook it warmly. "Don't get this way much. Guess you're right. The last time was about two years ago. Right after Beth turned five, if I recall right." His eyes started to move around the table but came to an abrupt halt when he saw Kate.

"Katherine. My God, Katherine, where have you been? What are you doing here? I've been searching for you for weeks." Garner rounded the table so fast that Kate had little time to digest the fact that he knew her. He started to draw her up into a hug but she flinched and he stopped, seeing her confusion, and wondering what was going on.

"I... I know you, don't I?" Kate wasn't sure what else to say.

"Well, I would hope so. You've known me for years." Garner smiled but couldn't keep the impatience out of his voice as he gazed down at the young woman, then at the faces around the room. What was going on here?

Ah hell, this couldn't get worse, Niall thought. His eyes shifted from Trent to Kate, who were staring at each other, one bewildered, and the other trying hard to match this man with her past. Trent. Wasn't her ring engraved with "Love, T?" This was her husband? *Trent Garner and Kate are husband and wife?* God, he was going to be ill. This couldn't be happening. Had he bedded the wife of a man he respected, and liked, more than any other man he knew? But she'd been a virgin, hadn't she? He couldn't be wrong about that.

"I do know you." Kate's voice started to rise as tears filled her eyes. She glanced at Alicia with a tentative smile and hope written all over her face. "Yes, yes, I do know who you are. Papa. Oh God, I remember you!" Kate flew into his arms, crying as she held tight to her father.

Papa? Not her husband? Niall was numb, staring at the two of them hugging, with Trent trying to calm his daughter down, offering words of encouragement, and saying everything would be okay. But Niall knew everything would not be okay. And it was his fault.

"It's all right, sweetheart. I've found you, and everything is going to be all right." Trent had a hard time keeping his voice from breaking down.

"Well, I'll be damned," Will said. "Kate is Marshal Garner's daughter. Who would've guessed?" He shook his head and sat back down to absorb the latest news.

While the scene played out in front of him, Jamie gazed around at the faces, trying to figure out how this young woman had found her way to the MacLaren ranch. A woman without a memory, without a last name, and she was now Beth's governess. There was a lot of explaining that needed to be done.

"Someone please tell me what is going on here," Jamie said to no one in particular.

"It's a long story, Jamie," Alicia offered. "Let me go into the kitchen a minute. I'll get you and Trent something to eat and explain everything."

Chapter Fifteen

"I can't believe how this whole thing played out." Trent was still incredulous at the turn of events. He'd found out Kate was missing a few weeks after her departure for California. He hadn't heard from her, but that wasn't unexpected as her trip was a long one, and she'd wanted to stop over in some of the towns during her journey. Then he figured she was getting settled in her new place and setting up the school.

Everything changed when he received the telegram from the school board saying Kate had never arrived. The only other time in his life he remembered feeling such panic was when his wife had taken ill, then died from her illness. He'd felt helpless, an emotion, that at the time, was new to him. This time he hadn't felt helpless. Trent knew he had the resources to find his daughter. His main concern had been in what condition he'd find her. But now Trent knew she was safe, and with one of the finest families he'd ever known. He thought of them as family and knew, with absolute certainty, the MacLarens had protected Kate, and not allowed anything or anyone to harm her.

"It's about as close to a miracle as I've ever seen, that's for sure." Alicia was picking up dessert plates and offering more coffee to the crowd around the table. No one had left, including Jocelyn, who sat alone, all but ignored.

Jocelyn had said little since Jamie and Trent had burst into the room. Her expression, however, had been anything but calm. At least twice during the commotion she'd tried to tug on Niall's arm to get him to continue, but all he did was tell her they'd discuss it later. Yes, Jocelyn was a very unhappy woman.

While everyone took turns explaining parts of the stagecoach wreck and Katherine's subsequent arrival at the ranch, Kate sat listening, staring at her father, and twisting the gold band. Her head whirled as she pieced together the events of her life. She was a teacher. It was a thrill to know her guesses about certain parts of her life had been correct. She now knew she'd been on her way to California, or at least she had been until the accident. Kate had no idea if the position was still available. Right now it seemed insignificant compared to the return of her memory and her father's arrival.

His arrival also helped ease the pain Kate felt about Niall. Her father could never find out. Nothing could be allowed to damage his relationship with the MacLarens. Even though neither she nor her mother had ever met them, it was well known her father was close to the family. Watching all of them together, it was obvious they felt the same about him. There was no reason for her to stay now that she was reclaiming her past. Niall had made it clear he could never love her, preferring Jocelyn's prospects and social standing to her. Her father might even insist she return East. The thought made Kate cringe. That wasn't what Kate wanted. She wanted to continue her life on her own terms, even if she wasn't sure what those terms were right now.

"Kate?" Niall stood before her, hands at his sides, discomfort in his eyes. Everyone else had gone outside, but Kate had been so lost in her thoughts she hadn't noticed. Niall knew Trent had lost his wife several years ago. He also knew Trent had a daughter, but he would never have connected this woman with his long-time friend. Niall had watched her throughout the telling of the accident that led to her becoming a "part of the family," as Alicia had phrased it. "Kate, I'd like to speak with you. What happened between us ..."

That was all he got out before Kate's eyes blazed and her hand came up as if to warn him off. "We don't need to speak of last night. I see no reason for it, Niall. Your lack of feelings for me, and your plans to wed without love, are quite clear." She looked away as if trying to organize her thoughts, before continuing. "But if you're worried about me saying anything to my father, rest assured I have no desire to cause him pain or drive a wedge between your family and him. He'll learn nothing from me. I plan to leave as soon as I find out if there's still a position for me in California. If not, I'll be leaving anyway. It's obvious I can no longer stay." Kate stood erect as she spoke to him, gazing into his striking green eyes. She'd miss those eyes, but she wouldn't miss the pain. She was going to forget Niall, forget he wanted another woman for his wife. Kate thought of him with Jocelyn, kissing her, making love to her the way he'd loved her last night. The image caused her stomach to twist into knots and produce a painful ache in the area of her heart. Yes, she'd forget this place and the bittersweet memories that came with it.

Niall watched her expressive face as she spoke. The words she said were true, but the impact on him was more painful than he ever would have imagined. He continued to gaze down at her as he fought his tangled emotions. He doubted she was even aware she continued to worry the band on her finger as she waited for his reply. That damned gold band. It had caused so much confusion. Now, of course, he knew Trent had given it to her when she left home. Almost like a talisman, it was a sign of her father's love, a token to keep her safe, and a part of her heritage. Her mother's wedding band. Trent felt certain it had played a part in getting her to the MacLaren's and keeping her safe until he found her.

"I understand. But I wasn't worried about you speaking with Trent." He stopped to look out the window when he heard someone call his name then turned back at Kate. "I need to take Jocelyn back to town," Niall said, "but would very much like to speak with you when I return." Her eyes provided him the answer before she responded. He didn't know why he was even pursuing this. He should be glad, relieved Trent had found his daughter and Kate had regained her memory. But something kept nagging at him. He didn't know what, but he knew it was important he figure it out, and soon.

"A couple of hours ago you were ready to offer marriage to another woman. We both know Jocelyn is who you want, not me. Knowing I'm Trent's daughter, and not married, changes nothing. You're a very tough man, Niall. You're tougher than the rest." She spoke these words in a soft voice, without rancor. "I envy you the ability to set a course of action and follow it through, no matter how your actions affect others. You don't love Jocelyn, but you'd sacrifice that for her social background. Beth can't stand the woman, but that's a small price to pay for the connections your marriage will produce. No, Niall, I'll not stand in the way of your carefully planned future. Marry her. It's obvious what you want from a marriage is nothing like what I will expect from mine." Kate didn't know how she got the words out as her heart was pounding so hard she could barely breathe. But it had been her heart that had gotten her into bed with Niall, and she'd no longer pay it any mind.

Niall continued to stare at Kate through eyes that had turned to slits. Her words were accurate, but they cut through him as if a knife had plunged into his chest. "All right, Kate, I won't press you. But there is more to this. You know it and so do I. Don't delude yourself—this isn't settled." Niall turned, walked through the front door, and climbed up onto the wagon for the trip to town.

Kate started out the door to find her father, letting Niall's final words settle in. "...don't delude yourself, this isn't settled." *Did I miss something when he told me he'd never love me? That he'd marry Jocelyn to further his ambitions?* Kate asked herself, as so many emotions crashed through her mind. No, Kate had no doubt the next time she saw Niall, he'd be betrothed to Jocelyn.

Both Kate and Niall had been so wrapped up in their own thoughts that neither noticed the person standing in the dining room, listening. *Well, that was interesting. This just keeps getting more intriguing.*

******

Jocelyn became increasingly agitated during the trip back to town. She was sure Niall would use this time, alone with her, to finish what he'd started after supper, but he was silent. The one time she broached the subject, he'd told her they'd talk about it later.

"No, Niall, we need to discuss this now," Jocelyn demanded as they arrived at her home in town. She didn't raise her voice, but her tone was set. "What were you going to say before we were interrupted? Were you proposing?"

Niall set the brake on the wagon before sitting back on the seat and staring up into the clear sky. He didn't know how to respond. His feelings for Kate had grown during her time at the ranch. He thought of her constantly, fighting the growing sense he should call everything off with Jocelyn. Last night wasn't so much a mistake as it was a true reflection of his desire and growing need for Kate. And Kate's parting words had shaken him. Was he sacrificing everything, including his daughter's feelings, for a woman he didn't even like in order to achieve some misguided need for political gain? "Jocelyn, I know this may be unfair to you, given the direction the conversation was headed at dinner, but right now I'm not ready to talk about us." He jumped off the wagon and walked around to assist Jocelyn down.

"I don't understand your hesitancy. If you planned to propose, how could the events of today change your mind? We've discussed the benefits of a union many times. Unless it's the girl. Is she the reason you're backing away?" Niall didn't answer, just watched as she continued her protest. "She's not right for you and has nothing to bring to a marriage. I don't understand how you could even consider someone like her when I have so much to offer."

He made no attempt to explain himself. His reasons for holding off were his own.

"Will I see you again, or is this good-bye?" Jocelyn had never been one to mince words.

"Let's leave it for now, all right? I plan to see you Sunday for dinner, unless you'd prefer I not come," he said in a matter-of-fact tone. He needed time to think, to figure out if the gnawing sensations in his stomach were from the fact he'd just learned Kate was Trent's daughter, or something more. If more, did it mean he had deeper feelings for Kate than he thought? That he might be in love with her? And, if he loved her, could he throw away everything he thought vital to go after her?

"Sunday dinner is fine, Niall. I will expect you after church." What else could Jocelyn say? She didn't love Niall, not in the least, but she wasn't ready to lose him, especially not to someone so far beneath her in wealth and standing. No, Niall would be hers. It would just take more time.

Chapter Sixteen

"So how did both of you happen to come to Fire Mountain? Were you working another case together?" Niall asked as they settled themselves next to the corral railing. Trent, Jamie, and Niall had disappeared to discuss the real reason Jamie had come to Fire Mountain.

"Actually, it was pure luck," Jamie responded. "I stopped at the sheriff's office in Phoenix to check-in, and there was Trent, asking about Kate, checking leads to her whereabouts."

"I had already been to the stage office," Trent interjected, "and although they don't keep names, the descriptions of the two women on the wrecked stage matched Kate and Mrs. Stelford. Sheriff said my best chance was to head to Fire Mountain, where some of the passengers were taken for medical treatment." Trent shook his head and laughed. "Small world. Jamie walks in just as the sheriff mentions Fire Mountain, and all he says is, 'Hey Garner. That's where I'm headed. We'll go together.' That's it. No, 'Hello, Trent. How're you doing?'" Trent laughed again. "All these years and Jamie is still the same pushy, pain-in-the-ass he was as a kid," Trent finished. Everyone smiled, especially Jamie.

"We decided to head to the ranch, get some food and sleep, then talk to Sheriff Rawlins tomorrow about Kate and the recent robberies," Jamie said.

Discovering Kate at the ranch had been so unexpected that the robberies had been forgotten.

Trent had agreed to help Jamie, but at the time, Kate had been his number one priority. Now that her whereabouts were known, Trent was free to devote some time to his friend and protégé, Jamie. The three men would go over what they knew so far, and then ride into town the next morning to meet with the sheriff and Sam.

"So no one's noticed anything more missing, right, Niall?" Jamie asked right off.

"Not that I'm aware of, unless something was taken last night during the dance, but I think it's unlikely," Niall replied. "The sheriff's plan to have everyone lock up their valuables got people's attention. Most ranchers left at least one man on watch, and many of the town's people took Atkinson up on his offer to store their jewelry in his fault. But we may not find out if anything is missing for several days. As you already know, only cash and jewelry have been taken, and darned little from each home. We found nothing broken and no clues. The lone way we can figure to flush them out is to have Hen's celebration, and invite enough people so we can watch their places with two or three ranchers and a few men from town. Of course the ranchers will have their men on watch, so we need to post our own people in town. Hen's having the party Wednesday, at his home. We need to settle on who's watching each place."

"Two men should be at each location," Trent interjected. "More men should be posted around town watching for anything out of the ordinary. These wouldn't be the law, but regular town folk that can be trusted. They wouldn't confront anyone, just report to one of us if they see anything suspicious. Do you think there are eight or ten men you'd trust to do this, Niall?"

"I don't know for sure that we can come up with that many. Most of the ones we know well will be at the party. None of us has the slightest idea who's behind this, so it's hard to know who to trust."

"Understood," Trent replied.

"What about here, Niall? Who'll be watching the house and women?" Jamie could volunteer to stay, but he felt his presence in town was more critical.

"Drew, Will, Gus, and Pete know what's happening, and will be watching out for everyone. We're okay here." At least Niall hoped they'd be safe. So far, no one had been hurt, but then no one had seen the thief, or thieves. He didn't know what would happen if someone confronted them during a robbery.

****

Kate hadn't spoken another word to Niall. It was Wednesday morning and she'd spent all her time with Trent or Beth. She helped Alicia prepare meals, rode Captain each afternoon, borrowed books from Niall's library when he was out of the house, and planned her day to avoid him. It was obvious, but there wasn't much he could do about it. Maybe it was for the best. He needed time to think, sort out what he thought he wanted from what he needed.

The more Niall rehashed the events of the last few weeks, the more he realized how he'd deliberately ignored what was happening between them. Niall knew he was attracted to Kate from that first encounter in Phoenix. His defenses had spiked right up. He'd built more walls each time since, pushed her away, and tried to convince himself that marrying Jocelyn was still what he wanted. But the truth was, he no longer believed it. All he could think about was Kate. She was beautiful, yes, but she was also compassionate, intelligent, and funny. He'd witnessed her humor, even though it had rarely been directed at him. She'd become important to Beth, and if he were honest, important to him. He'd been a bastard from the start, pushing her away every chance he got.

His instincts told him she was at least a little in love with him. He'd taken those feelings and crushed them, declared he'd never be able to love her. But he wanted her. Hell, he wanted her with an intensity that surprised him. He doubted she'd give him a chance, let him make-up for the wrongs already committed. But he needed to try, and Niall knew he'd never be free to work things out with Kate until she believed Jocelyn was firmly in his past.

******

"Are you going to tell me what's wrong, Katherine, or keep me wondering for a few more days?" Trent had always been able to read his daughter. She was hiding something, but he couldn't figure out what. Kate was an open book most of the time. She didn't hide her feelings and never played the mind games many women enjoyed.

But now she was holding something back and he was determined to discover it.

"I don't know what you mean. Everything is wonderful now that you're here and my memory has returned." *Darn it*, Kate thought. She knew her father could see right through her. She'd been trying to keep her feelings for Niall, and the events of the past weekend, out of her thoughts. What had betrayed her? She'd asked this question many times during her life, but this time it was so much more important to keep what had transpired from her father.

Trent knew a cover-up when he saw one, and Katherine was covering in a major way. Fine, he'd be patient. History told him she couldn't keep this up for long. She'd slip and give him the opportunity he needed to find out what was eating at her.

"All right, if that's the way you want it, I'll back away for now. But you and I both know it's simply a matter of time before you realize you can tell me. You'll tell me because you know I'll help you through it, no matter what it is."

Darn, darn, darn. Well, what had she expected? A confrontation with her father might be inevitable, but she wouldn't deal with it today. "You'll wait a long time, because you're just imagining something."

"Is this a private discussion, or may I join the two of you?" Alicia had spent much of the morning baking for Hen and Anna's anniversary party that evening. She'd known them since they'd arrived in Fire Mountain not long after she'd married Stuart. At one point everyone thought their daughter,

Victoria, would marry Jamie. The two had become engaged right before Jamie had left on a cattle drive. But a newcomer to town had convinced Victoria to marry, and before anyone knew what was happening, she and the stranger had wed and left Fire Mountain. Jamie returned to town to hear the news from Hen. There was no message from Victoria as to why. She was just gone. No one had heard much from them after that, other than to learn Victoria and her husband had settled in San Francisco.

The unanticipated marriage had devastated not only Hen and Anna, but also Jamie. He and Niall argued several times after she left. The arguments, combined with Victoria's betrayal had pushed Jamie to leave the ranch for New Mexico, and eventually, through the encouragement of Trent Garner, to join the U.S. Marshals Service. Alicia hoped that perhaps the time had come for Niall and Jamie to work through their past differences.

"Not private at all, Alicia. Katherine has seemed pretty quiet the last couple of days, and I was attempting to get her to share her thoughts." Perhaps Alicia would join him in trying to get Kate to open up.

"Well, I'm sure Kate will talk about what's bothering her when she's ready, right, honey?" She looked at Kate and smiled, but Alicia also wondered when, or if, the girl would discuss what ate at her.

"Of course, Alicia, but there's nothing to talk about. Papa worries too much."

"Yes, well, it seems for good reason," Trent mumbled as he busied himself with packing some of the baked goods.

"Kate, you sure you don't mind staying with Beth while I go to the party with Jamie and Niall? I don't have to go." Alicia hated leaving Kate, but she suspected the young woman could use some time alone at the house to gather her thoughts and decide her future. No one was sure if she'd stay on as Beth's governess, or contact the school in California to see if the original position was still available.

"Actually Alicia, I'm looking forward to some time to myself once Beth goes to bed. I know Drew and Will are planning to stay, so we won't be alone. Besides, I promised Beth I'd help her work on a vest for riding." Kate loved Beth and their time together had become more special than she cared to admit.

"All right then. We'll be leaving soon and won't return until close to ten." Alicia left to finish her preparations. Trent gave his daughter a kiss on the cheek and a meaningful glance before excusing himself to find Jamie.

Kate sat alone with her conflicting thoughts. She needed to make some decisions, and they needed to be made soon.

******

"What's going on with you and Kate? The tension between the two of you is crushing, and it's apparent you're avoiding each other." Jamie had always been direct and tended to insert himself into situations that were none of his business. Niall knew those same traits were also what made him an exceptional lawman.

"Don't know what you mean, Jamie. Kate is Beth's governess, so we talk some most days. And about the tension—you're imaging it."

"Hell, Niall, don't lie to me. I know there's something going on. If I didn't know better I'd think the two of you were involved, maybe real involved." Jamie's eyes bored into Niall's, searching for the truth. He knew he was pushing, but something was going on between Niall and the daughter of his mentor, a father figure, and he didn't want Niall doing anything to damage the relationship.

"Drop it, Jamie. It's none of your business," Niall glared right back at him.

"Ah, shit, Niall, you're sleeping with her, aren't you? You son of a bitch, what are you thinking? She's Trent's daughter and you're bedding her? Does anyone else have any idea what's going on or am I the only one who's stumbled on it?" Jamie stood in Niall's space, his temper escalating as well as his voice.

"Damn it Jamie, it's not what you think. I didn't even know she was Trent's daughter until Sunday. No one even knew her last name."

"And now¬¬¬¬¬¬¬¬¬¬¬?" Jamie wouldn't let up.

"And now? The truth is Kate can't stand the sight of me. She puts up with me because she loves Beth, and because there was nowhere else for her to go until she regained her memory. Now that she has, the odds are she won't stay. It will devastate Beth, but Kate has her life back and will do what she's got to do." Niall ran a hand through his dark hair then scrubbed at his face.

He couldn't let Jamie know he'd bedded Kate, taken her virginity. Jamie would go wild, and it would accomplish nothing but taint a beautiful young woman whom Niall happened to care about a great deal. It wasn't her fault he'd sought her out and seduced her. He'd known when he entered her room he could persuade her. Her strong feelings for him had been obvious, and in hindsight, he'd exploited them. What made him even more of a bastard was that he'd thought she was married, and still he went to her. His desire for her had been too strong, his need for her too great. He'd been weak, and given in to those feelings, hurting someone he now realized he cared about deeply, but who might now be out of his reach forever because of his selfish actions.

"Swear to me nothing has happened between you and Kate, Niall."

"I've said all I'm going to say about it, Jamie." Niall turned to go. Jamie reached out, grabbed his arm, and spun him around.

"Swear, damn it." Jamie exploded, his rage getting the better of him.

The punch to his jaw came so fast that Jamie had no time to react. It spun him sideways, but his reflexes were quick as he shot a fist straight into Niall's stomach. Niall bent over trying to catch his breath. Jamie landed another blow to his face and Niall fell to his back.

"What's going on in here? Are you two loco?" Gus bellowed as he walked over and knelt next to

Niall to survey the damage. "Get your butt over here, Jamie, and help your brother up. Home a few days and already you two are at each other. Alicia's going to have a fit." Gus couldn't hide his disgust. Three damn days and they were back to fighting. When they were younger, Stuart would have thrown both of them into the water trough, but that wouldn't work any longer. They were men and had to work out the anger between them on their own. Thank God, neither was bleeding. There'd be bruises, but those they'd be able to hide. Blood would be another matter.

Niall was up, brushing himself off while Jamie located his hat and pressed it back on his head. Neither spoke, just continued to glare at each other. Disgusted, Jamie turned first and walked out of the barn, and right into Trent. One look from Jamie silenced him. He glanced at Niall. *Well, something happened*, Trent thought, but he wasn't about to get into the middle of at it at this point. Whatever had set them off was still hanging out there. This wasn't the end of it, that was for darn certain.

Chapter Seventeen

The celebration in town was a success by anyone's measure. Hen and Anna had a wonderful anniversary, and Trent spotted someone entering the Riley residence about an hour into the party. The intruder didn't see Trent standing in the shadows of a house across the street as he opened a side window and climbed through with little effort. Whoever he was, he was slight of stature and nimble.

Trent motioned to Niall as he came up the street, and together they hustled to the Riley's, Niall standing outside the window while Trent went through the back door. Trent could hear movement upstairs. He snuck up the steps as he drew his revolver from its holster without making a sound. Luck was with him. He was able to get to the landing without the stairs squeaking to give him away. He rounded a corner and was staring right at the thief, who was rifling through a box of jewelry and pocketing a couple of items. *I've got you*, the marshal thought. He raised his gun.

"Hold it there, mister, and raise your hands." Before Trent knew what was happening, the intruder turned, ran at him, and dodged right past, elbowing him while knocking him against a wall. Trent recovered and sent a warning yell to Niall, who jumped through the window and caught the thief head-on. Tackling him, Niall attempted to secure his arms behind him, but a kick to the stomach forced Niall to turn the thief over and plant one solid blow to his face before the intruder surrendered. By then Trent was beside them, turned the thief over onto his stomach, clamped handcuffs on him, then turned him back to face them.

"You recognize him, Niall?"

That's when they both realized what they were looking at wasn't man, or a boy, but a young woman. How had they missed that? Her hair was secured on her head with a cap pulled snug on top. It's a wonder it hadn't come off in the fracas.

"Never saw her before," Niall replied, still in shock. "Christ, Trent. I slugged her damn hard after she kicked me. Can't be more than fourteen or fifteen, do you think?"

"Doesn't appear to be, but it's dark. Let's get her up and out of here, then head for the jail. We'll let Sam have a try at finding out what's going on. I'd appreciate it if you'd get Doc Minton to come and check her out." Trent had seen plenty of young boys and girls turn to crime out of desperation. Most stole food, clothing, and blankets. He couldn't remember a time he'd heard of them breaking into homes for jewelry. Stealing cash, yes, and begging or pick pocketing, as they sought enough change to eat.

Neither Sam nor Sheriff Rawlins recognized the girl, and neither did Doc when he arrived a few minutes later. She'd gained consciousness but refused to talk. The thief glared at each man in turn, then rolled to her side, ignoring them.

"What do you plan to do with her, Sheriff?" Niall asked as the men walked to the front office area.

"Think I'll get Reverend Blanchard and his wife over here. See if they recognize her, get her to talk some. I don't believe she's local but sure as hell don't know how she'd come to be here unless she was traveling with someone. You boys find anything else on her besides what she took tonight?" The sheriff looked at Trent and Niall.

The men just shook their heads.

"All right, then. I'll go get the Reverend. Try not to let her escape while I'm gone, boys," the sheriff drawled as he headed out the door.

"Why do you think she'd take jewelry, Trent? I can understand the cash, for food and such, but jewelry? What would she do with it?" Sam leaned back in his chair, lacing his fingers behind his head and closing his eyes, as if trying to figure out a puzzle.

Trent leaned his large frame against the deputy's desk and crossed his arms. "Don't know, Sam, unless she already has a buyer somewhere." He paused to ponder what he knew. "Except, if she needed the money, why would she leave any of the cash at each place? Makes little sense to me." He uncrossed his arms and pushed away from the desk.

"One thing's for sure," Sam continued. "She's going to tell us her story, or she'll stay in jail until she does."

Trent and Niall regarded Sam, then smiled at each other. Sam's doggedness was what made him

143

an exceptional deputy. They both knew if anyone could get her to open up it would be Sam.

******

Niall and Trent sat out on the porch the following night, drinking coffee and talking between themselves. "What are your plans now, Trent?"

"Fact is, I'm retiring at the end of the month. I've been doing this for over twenty years, which is long enough for any man. I think I'll take up ranching." Trent said, not looking at Niall, but gazing up at the stars on what was a beautiful northern Arizona night.

"Ranching, huh? Didn't know you ever had a desire to do that. What kind of ranching? Where?" A future with Kate might still be possible if Niall could talk Trent into settling down near Fire Mountain.

Trent kept staring up and smiled. "Well, I already own a place. I bought it before Stuart died. He helped me pick it out, negotiate the deal, and hire a foreman to run it. Man's done an excellent job the last few years. I'm hoping he'll stay around."

"Here? Your place is here in Fire Mountain?" How did Niall not know this? He knew all the ranchers and all the spreads.

"It's the old Parson place. Butts up to your property on the east," Trent explained as if the information was insignificant. Niall was stunned at the news.

"Well, I'll be damned. I heard some rich easterner bought the place and hired Josh Jacklin to run it. Never occurred to me it was you, and I never

144

asked Josh." Niall couldn't contain how much this pleased him.

"Well, I'm not wealthy, but my wife comes from money. It came to me when she died. We'd talked about a place out here for years but hadn't done anything. Before she died I promised I'd go ahead with our plans, and I did, but never had the heart to move into the place without her. Now it's time and I'm hoping Katherine will stay with me, at least for a while. By the way, doesn't the van Deelin place run along your border?"

"That it does, for quite a ways north of yours. It's good property, too, with water and excellent grass."

"Got to say, I was surprised to see Mrs. van Deelin at your place when we arrived. What was she doing there anyway?" He glanced over at Niall, knowing full well what Niall had planned. It had taken Will one day before he'd laid out the whole courting story to Trent, including the fact that no one, especially Beth, liked Jocelyn. They'd all been hoping something would develop between Kate and Niall. Trent's reaction to that had been surprise, but truth be told, he thought it a terrific idea.

"Well, I guess it's no real secret." Niall muttered.

"What's that?" Trent enjoyed Niall's discomfort.

"Damn, Trent, I'd planned to ask Jocelyn to marry me. We'd combine our lands and money, and grow the ranch. Seemed like a good idea—my land and ranching skills, her land and political connections. Now, well, I just don't know."

"And love?"

"Not a stitch. It'd be a business arrangement with no emotions involved. I loved Camille and have no interest in living through that kind of pain again. No, Trent, I have no feelings for Jocelyn and she has none for me." He shook his head and thanked God the past week had happened. Now that he'd accepted his deep affection for Kate, he didn't see how he could go through with his intent to marry Jocelyn. But, he owed it to Jocelyn to tell her before he told anyone else.

"What changed your mind?"

"Well, you and Jamie showed up when I was about to propose. That's why she came over to the house for dinner on Sunday. I was seconds away from making what could've been an enormous mistake, but again, you saved me." He smiled, stood from the chair, and walked to the porch rail. Niall asked himself how he could've been so blind to so many things the last few weeks. Was there any bigger fool?

"Hmm, I see. So that was it? We walked in and you changed your mind, just like that?" Trent knew there had to be more to it. Could this be at all related to what was going on with Katherine? His gut told him there had to be a connection between Niall's change of mind and his daughter.

"Not exactly. Other things entered into it, too. I had doubts even as I was about to ask her. Your arrival, and Kate regaining her memory, made me realize I wasn't quite ready to go through with it. There were other things I wanted." Niall hoped he hadn't said too much. Kate still avoided him and he had no doubt this would continue for a while.

"And what's that, Niall?"

"Trent, Niall, I'm headed to bed. Anything more you two want?"

Niall breathed a sigh of relief. *Thank you, Aunt Alicia.* She may have just saved him from Trent's continued questions. "Nothing more for me. I'll follow you up as I have another long day tomorrow. Trent, I'll see you in the morning."

"I'll see you in the morning then, Niall. Goodnight, Alicia." Trent knew this conversation would continue another time. He'd bet money Niall's change of plans and Katherine's continued silence were connected. He needed to find out how.

Chapter Eighteen

"Here? You own a ranch here, in Fire Mountain?" Kate couldn't hide her surprise. A ranch in Fire Mountain could mean she might be able to work out some type of arrangement to stay as Beth's governess. At least if Alicia made the decision. She knew Alicia didn't want her to leave and concocted all manner of schemes to entice her to stay.

"Right here, Katherine. Our land shares a portion of the east property line with the MacLaren spread. It takes a while to go between the two by buggy or wagon, but by horse it's a short ride." Trent could see the excitement in his daughter's face.

"When can I see it?"

"Today, if you'd like. I saw our foreman, Josh Jacklin, in town, and told him to expect us. He's got the house open and had someone come out to clean. Nothing fancy. I'm sure there'll be things to do before we move in. Maybe you'll like it enough to consider staying with your old man." Trent didn't want to get his hopes up, but he did want Katherine to consider staying on for at least awhile, maybe forever if she met someone and got married. Niall's image broke into his thoughts.

"Today is great. I'll go change so we can ride over as soon as you want." Kate was out the door before Trent could answer. *That went well*, Trent thought as he donned his hat and made his way outside to saddle their horses.

He met Niall in the barn, going over a supply list with Gus. Trent grabbed his gear and headed for Champion, a large appaloosa he'd owned for many years. They'd been partners enforcing the law, and now they'd be partners on his ranch.

"Going someplace, Trent?" Niall finished up with Gus and walked over to Champion, running his hand down the large flanks and admiring the horse's lines. This was one fine horse.

"Katherine and I are riding over to my place to meet with Josh. She's quite anxious to see it."

"Mind if I tag along?" No way would Niall let Kate come face to face with Josh Jacklin before he had a chance to talk with her. What better way to start than during a ride to Trent's place? Plus, Josh had a reputation with the women that rivaled anyone else's. Tall, lean but muscular, Josh had dark blonde hair and a slow, easy manner that was deceiving. People thought he was a little slow in some things, but Niall knew different. Josh was as sharp as they came. He possessed a good eye for stock, both cows and horses, had a savvy business mind, managed the men well, and had a good reputation for running a clean operation. And women practically threw themselves at him. Nope, he was definitely riding over with them.

"Okay by me." Trent had to suppress a smile. He had a pretty good idea what was going through Niall's mind. Trent already knew about Josh's reputation with the ladies, and if something was going on between Niall and his daughter, Niall wouldn't want Josh anywhere near Katherine. Plus, this would give Trent a chance to see how Katherine and Niall interacted. He'd been surprised at how little they'd spoken since his arrival, but perhaps that was normal. His gut told him otherwise. Yes, this could be the perfect opportunity to see if he could determine what was troubling his daughter and if it involved the oldest MacLaren.

"Ready?" Kate rushed into the barn. She was eager to see the ranch and hear her father's plans.

"Niall's saddling up now." Trent saw Katherine's smile fade but ignored it. Whatever was going on between them would work itself out, one way or another.

"He's going with us?" Kate wasn't up for a day with Niall. They'd spoken little the past week, and only when necessary. From what she could tell he hadn't asked Jocelyn to marry him, but she knew it was simply a matter of time. It was too painful to be around him. She knew the hurt would fade, but what she needed now was space.

"Yes. Is there a problem with that?"

"Uh, no, it's fine." Kate's enthusiasm had lessened in just a few seconds. She had to get over it. Niall was, after all, her employer, and she did want to keep her job if she stayed in Fire Mountain.

Niall rode up from the back of the barn, met the others, and tipped his hat to Kate. "Hello, Kate. You don't mind if I join you, do you?" He hoped to get a conversation going with her, but she just shook her head in response. "All right. Let's get going."

They rode in silence for most of the trip. Kate held back, several yards behind the two men. She needed to come to terms with her feelings for the oldest MacLaren, accept that he'd never be hers, and go on with her life. Maybe find someone else who could fill her thoughts, and with time, her heart. Niall wasn't the only man she could love, was he?

Niall wanted nothing more than to ride beside Kate, but she refused to nudge Captain forward. Trent made it a point to ferry between the two during the short ride, and encouraged Niall to drop back with him, but when he tried, she slowed her horse even more. It was obvious Kate wanted no part of him. He'd have to find a way to get her to talk with him, about anything. He needed to hear her voice, her laugh, and to see her smile.

Niall pointed out various landmarks, watering areas, and places where cows liked to disappear. These were long expanses of large rock formations and narrow valleys. "Cows wander into these areas. It takes a good deal of patience to locate them. But, I'm sure Josh will go over all this with you if he hasn't already." Niall knew a lot about Trent, but not the least about his knowledge of running a ranch.

"Tell you what, Niall. You're welcome to tutor me whenever you have the time. I worked my folks place in Texas until I left to join the marshals. Since then, nothing. I'm an open book." Trent knew when he needed to follow the guidance of others, and he thanked his friend Stuart, Niall's uncle, for helping him find this place and hire Jacklin.

"Well, Josh is a good man, one of the best. Tried to hire him away a few times, but he refused to budge."

"Yeah, Josh told me about those times. Hard to find loyal men, but he sure seems to be one of them." Trent laughed, recalling each time a message from Josh would arrive saying MacLaren had offered him another position. Trent made sure to pay him what Niall offered and gave Josh a free hand to run the ranch. Not much more a foreman could ask from his boss.

"It isn't much further to our place, Katherine. A few more minutes and we'll be on Garner land," her father said as they continued around an area of rocks and trees. There wasn't as much cactus as Kate had imagined. Pines and scrub oak were more prevalent at this elevation.

They rode over one last hill and were starting down when Niall reined in Zeus. "This is it. The Garner ranch," he said to Trent and Kate as they joined him.

The Garner ranch. The thought of it gave Kate chills. All this time and she had no idea her father had purchased land to practice his second profession. The thought of him being away from the constant danger that was expected as a marshal was a tremendous relief. She and her mother had always supported his chosen job, but it was good to see him leave it behind and settle in one place. And a beautiful place at that, where she could join him.

It wasn't much longer before a white house appeared in the distance with a barn not far behind it. Out buildings, one that appeared to be a bunkhouse, were off to the left. Horses grazed from piles of hay in a couple of corrals near the barn. The trio had reached the house when a tall, very good-looking man came out from around a corner and walked up to them.

"Trent, how are you doing?" The man extended his hand to her father.

"Great, Josh, glad to be here. Thought I'd show off the place to my daughter, Katherine, and Niall MacLaren, whom I'm sure you know. Katherine, this is Josh Jacklin, our foreman. Josh, my daughter, Katherine."

Josh tipped his hat, "Glad to meet you, Katherine."

"Kate, please, Mr. Jacklin."

"Kate is fine, but you'll need to call me Josh." He finished with a broad smile of flawless, straight, white teeth.

Yes indeed, he's definitely handsome, Kate thought.

Niall dismounted and walked between Kate and Josh, extending his hand to Josh as he blocked the man's view of Kate, who was leading her horse to the water trough.

"How are you, Josh? Haven't seen you since the last ranchers' meeting."

"Good, Niall, I'm good." Josh tried to lean around Niall for a better view of Kate. *Not happening, friend*, Niall thought as he turned to follow Kate to the trough. Sensing there was more to this than he understood, Josh took the safe approach and offered to show them the house first, then anything else they wanted to see.

Kate found the house clean, if sparse, with three bedrooms upstairs, a decent sized kitchen, small dining room, and large living room. There was

153

another room used as an office, plus a storage room off the kitchen. She liked it immediately, and was already making plans to spruce it up.

"Tell me how everything is going," Trent requested as they sat at a small table in the dining room. Josh poured coffee for all of them and took a seat next to Kate.

"You know pretty much all of it, Trent. Herd's growing, we had a good summer, and are prepared for the weather that'll be moving in over the next few months. Bought the other bull you wanted. He sure has been a busy guy, from what we can tell." Josh glanced over at Kate, "Uh, sorry, ma'am."

"No problem, Josh. I'm pretty sure I know how calves are created." Did she just say that, with Niall sitting right across from her? She glanced up, and sure enough, he had the nerve to look straight at her and smile. Kate knew she must be blushing, but she turned more towards Josh and ignored Niall's laughing eyes. Trent took this all in, but said nothing.

"Uh, yes, ma'am," Josh answered. "Anyway, with the new bull and the one we already have, we should have a real good crop of new calves this spring. We're all looking forward to it. The boys are getting ready to work some of the new horses and separate the best cow ponies. We've got some real good wranglers, Trent, best we've had in three years. Our reputation is spreading and they're starting to come to us rather than me beating the bushes for men not already taken by the bigger spreads. Begging your pardon, of course, Niall." Josh stopped to sip his coffee before continuing.

"No problem, Josh. I know it's difficult for the smaller places to hire good people and I'm glad you've got a good group this year." Having a successful ranch right next to his meant better conditions for everyone, in Niall's opinion.

"One guy is giving me problems though, and I need to cut him loose soon. We're about one or two men heavy going into winter anyway, so I should do it now before we get any closer. Give him a chance to find something else." It was clear Josh put a lot of thought into working with the ranch hands and understood their nomadic life style.

"That's your call, Josh. However you want to handle it is fine." Trent had been more than satisfied over the years with Josh's approach to handling the ranch and the men. "Katherine and I plan to start setting the house up, but won't move in for a couple of weeks. I received a telegram saying the Marshals Service is transferring my work to a new captain. They're letting me go a little early, which suits me fine." Trent's smile was broad. His relief at not having to report back to process any final assignments was evident. He'd given them a good, long turn, and now it was time to move on.

"You're moving in too, Kate?" Josh asked, somewhat surprised, but pleased. "That's great. A woman's touch around here is exactly what this place needs. Don't you think so, Niall?" He cast a knowing look in Niall's direction. It was obvious Josh was catching the under currents between Niall and Kate, the same as Trent.

"Yeah, Josh, a woman's touch would be good." Niall was more than ready to head back and get

Kate as far away from Josh as possible. He needed to come up with a solution to the mess he'd made of his life, and fast. The last thing he needed was competition from Garner's foreman.

Chapter Nineteen

"All we can find out is she's not from here. Won't give us her name or age, or if she has any kin nearby," Sam said. Niall and Trent had stopped by the sheriff's office to check out the girl, see if she was doing all right, and if they knew anything more about her or the thefts. Sam stared at the cells behind him and continued in a soft voice filled with frustration. "But, I'm pretty sure she has a brother."

"Is that so?" Trent asked as he removed his hat and sat down in the one of the offered chairs.

"You won't believe it, but Gloria Chalmette, you know her, Niall, from the Desert Dove down the street?" Sam paused a second, but Niall merely nodded. "Well, she stopped by a few days ago saying there's this boy, maybe ten or eleven, who keeps stopping by, asking for work. But he's also checking to see if anyone's seen a girl, about fourteen, with sandy blonde hair and brown eyes. You know Gloria can't turn a hungry kid away, so she feeds him, but he won't open up much. Always mentions this girl, and when no one offers information, he takes off. He's done that three or four times now. She figures he's due back today, maybe tomorrow, if his pattern holds true."

"Sounds to me like someone should be down at the Dove, watching for him," Trent interjected as he thought about another child being involved in the thefts. "Anything else missing that you know of, Sam?"

"Not a thing. Since she's been in here a few days, nothing's been reported. But it's got me thinking we may have ourselves a hungry family camped or living somewhere outside of town. Send their kids into town to steal, and then the adults come in and buy the food." Puzzles had always been of interest to Sam, and this one sure was a puzzle.

"As good a guess as any, I suppose. Niall, you want to head down to the Dove, check around, and speak with this Gloria woman?" Trent asked.

"Uh, why don't I do that, Trent," Sam spoke up. "I'll grab something to eat, hang around, and see if the boy shows."

"Sounds good to me." Niall glanced at Sam and nodded, knowing the deputy was trying to help a touchy situation. He hadn't seen Gloria since the night he'd been with Kate. He had no desire to be with anyone else, couldn't work up the enthusiasm or desire. Niall knew Gloria would be hurt, but he couldn't risk being seen with her at the Dove if there was to be anything between him and Kate. "I can stay here with the girl if you have things to do, Trent, or you can go with Sam."

"Guess I'll tag along with you, Sam. Meet this Gloria woman I've heard so much about over the years." With that last remark, he cast a meaningful glance at Niall and then headed out the door.

Hell, Niall thought. *He must have heard about her from Jamie, or maybe Sheriff Rawlins. Just can't keep secrets in small towns.*

******

158

"There he is, Sam, leaning around the corner at the back of the bar, near Ross." Gloria nodded in the boy's direction. Sam and Trent had taken a seat at a corner table so they could watch the doors, but each had missed the small figure already hiding in the saloon.

"So, how do you want to handle this, Sam?" Trent sipped his whiskey while gazing over the rim of his glass at the deputy.

"I'm thinking it best if you talk to him. You're not the law anymore. Maybe he'll open up to you."

"Sure. It's worth a try." The ex-marshal pushed himself up from the table and sauntered to the bar, following Gloria. He rested his arms on the bar, signaled to Ross for another drink, then waited to see what would happen.

About ten minutes later, the boy emerged, approached Trent with purposeful steps, and then stopped to look up at the big man.

"Hey, mister?"

"Yes, son, what can I do for you?" Trent smiled down at the small figure. The boy couldn't be more than ten, with the same sandy blonde hair as the girl in the jail. His clothes were dirty and his shoes ragged with holes, but his eyes were clear.

"Wondered if maybe you've seen a girl with blonde hair kind of like mine anywhere in town?"

"I might have. Why do you ask?"

"You saw her? Where at?" The boy tried to contain his excitement, but failed.

"I said I might have seen her. What do you want her for, son? Is she your kin?"

159

"That's my business, mister," the boy said, a hint of defiance in his voice.

"Well, then, I guess I haven't seen her," Trent countered, and set his glass down on the bar. "Thanks, Ross. See you later," he called to the bartender. He looked at the boy for a moment, and turned to leave.

Seeing his opportunity vanish, the boy ran after him. "Wait, mister. I have to find her," the boy called as he tried to catch the fast-walking, long-legged man.

"Then I guess you'll have to tell me why, son, 'cause I'm not telling you about her until I know more."

The boy hesitated a mere moment this time. "She's my sister. We got separated and I can't find her anywhere. It's been a few days." The poor kid sounded desperate, but Trent still wanted more information.

"Where's your family?"

"It's just my Ma, sister, and me. That's all." He stopped as if he didn't know if he should say any more.

"And where is your Ma? You're not from around here, are you, son?"

"No, sir. We were headed to California when our wagon broke down. Then Ma got sick and we ran out of food. I've been trying to get work at the saloon. Miss Gloria is nice and all, but she says a saloon is no place for a boy." He lowered his head as tears began to form in his eyes.

"Where's your Ma now?"

"We found an abandoned shack a couple of miles out of town. As soon as Ma gets better, and I find Alma, then we can take off again."

"Alma. That's your sister?" The boy nodded. Trent was glad to put a name with a face. "And your name?"

"Thomas, but Ma and Alma call me Tommy," he said before his eyes shifted back up at the stranger.

"All right, Tommy. Let's go find Alma." Trent smiled as he started to walk with Tommy to the jail.

Chapter Twenty

"Hey, Niall. What brings you out here?" Trent called out as his friend rode up to the barn.

"Riding over to Donovan's spread. Thought I'd stop for a minute since your ranch is on the way, see how much progress you've made for your move." Niall dismounted Zeus and led him to the water trough. "Been out with the boys all morning and could sure use a cup of coffee, if it's not too much trouble."

"Course not. I was heading that way myself. If we're lucky, Kate may have some food waiting." Trent smiled and slapped Niall on the back.

"Kate, we've got company," Trent called as he entered the kitchen.

"Company? But we haven't moved in yet," Kate called back. Then she saw the man standing behind her father. "Oh, hello, Niall." She hung a towel on a hook and placed the last bowl on the table.

"Kate. It's good to see you." Niall's breath caught as he took in the sight of her. He'd been out on their property most days this week and hadn't encountered her more than once or twice, and that only in passing. Seeing her now, hair piled on her head with a few loose strands falling down her neck and face, he realized he would never tire of looking at her.

"You'll join us for dinner, won't you?" Kate wanted him to refuse. She was doing better, coming to terms with his decision to marry Jocelyn. She didn't want to spend Saturday dinner with him.

"If it's not too much trouble, that would be great," he said, still taking in her image. "You've accomplished a lot in a few days, Kate. I guess it won't take long to get settled once you bring your things over from the ranch." He knew his attempts at small talk were pathetic. Their brief encounters at his ranch were made up of polite comments and stilted conversation. It wasn't enough.

"Well, you and Papa go ahead. I ate earlier, and was just headed out to get Captain," she lied. "Enjoy your day, Niall. Papa, I'll see you in a little bit." Kate kissed Trent on the check before gathering her hat and gloves to head for the barn.

Niall stood, staring after her. He'd come here specifically to see Kate. He wasn't riding to the Donovan ranch at all. It was an excuse to be around her, maybe talk with her a little.

"Guess you're going to have to try something else, son." Trent chuckled as he filled his plate.

Niall turned to look at him, ready to deny what Trent implied, but gave up, exhaling a deep breath he hadn't realized he was holding. "Ah, hell, Trent. I don't know what to do, what to think. She avoids me, won't speak to me other than polite conversation, and rides off each day as soon as she's done with Beth. All I want is some time to be around her, figure some things out."

"And what is it you need to figure out?" Trent had known Niall for almost fifteen years. He was like family, like a son. His affection for the MacLarens couldn't be stronger, and he'd be thrilled if Katherine took to Niall. He thought she already had, but understood her hesitancy, believing that he was determined to marry for reasons other than love.

"Just realizing I may be making an enormous mistake if I marry Jocelyn. But I can't get over the sense I'd be letting my family down if I don't make the most of the opportunity with her." He stopped long enough to shovel food into his mouth, and smiled. "She's a good cook, isn't she?" Niall asked on a swallow.

"That she is," Trent said, forging ahead when Niall didn't continue. "And how would you be letting your family down by not marrying Jocelyn?"

"I'm the oldest. I need to set things up so the ranch will continue to grow, be successful. Jocelyn has connections, money, everything we need to ensure success as the territory grows."

"But you don't love her."

"No, I don't love her. And she doesn't love me. Like I said before, it would be a marriage of convenience to further the interests of the MacLarens, as well as Jocelyn's dreams. She's an ambitious woman—has her eye on the governor's house. She thinks I don't know her goals, but I do. She believes I could take her there, but that's not what I want and never has been. She's easy to read, and there's no way I could ever love that woman." Niall lowered his head to take a few more bites of food.

"And how does my daughter play into this? Is she just a distraction, someone to focus on while you make a final decision on Jocelyn? 'Cause I got to tell you, son, if you decide you want Katherine, then break her heart, I may have to break your neck." The

164

last was said in a quiet tone, but there was pure steel behind the words.

Niall stopped to set his fork down and straighten in his seat. He wanted Kate. That was the absolute truth. Hadn't been able to get her off his mind since their night together. But was he certain he was in love with her? If he decided to go after Kate, and it didn't work out, he'd put the strongest bond he had, outside the family, to a severe test.

"I won't lie to you. I don't know that I can ever love again, after Camille. She meant everything to me. You understand. You were around us before she died. Don't know if a love like that can ever be replaced." The sadness in his voice was still apparent after all these years. "But I care a great deal for Kate, more than I ever thought I could. She's everything I'd want if I were to love again. I just don't know that I can promise it."

Trent took a few minutes to finish his dinner and let Niall's words play in his mind. He knew his daughter had feelings for this man, strong feelings, but she didn't want her father to know it. There wasn't much advice he could give these young people. He knew from experience they'd have to work through this on their own.

"Seems to me you have some thinking to do. She's not going anywhere, and spends five days a week at your place. If anyone has a chance to win her heart, it's you. That is, if you decide you want it. But if you don't, then stay away from her."

******

"Niall, you coming home to dinner today?" Aunt Alicia asked after church on Sunday. "Trent and Kate have decided to eat with us, then they'll be leaving for their ranch. Looks like it'll be their last day here." Alicia was sad, but still hopeful something might develop between her nephew and Trent's daughter, assuming Niall didn't decide to ask Jocelyn to marry him. The thought made her wince.

"Can't make it today, Aunt Alicia. Beth and I are going over to Jocelyn's for dinner. I'm sure I'll see them later in the week." More than anything, Niall wanted to spend the day around Kate. His heart told him to go home, spend time with her. His mind told him he owed it to the future of his family to confirm the decision he'd made was right.

Chapter Twenty-One

Jocelyn answered the knock in her most beautiful day dress. It was deep apricot, appropriately designed and form fitting, with a slight bustle. The brooch she wore was expensive, as were the matching earrings. The cook had outdone herself and Jocelyn planned to be the perfect hostess while reminding him of what he would lose if he walked away.

"Good afternoon, Jocelyn," Niall said as she opened the door and let the two guests move past her into the elegant foyer.

"Niall, it's good to see you." Jocelyn smiled but tempered her enthusiasm, waiting to see how the afternoon would unfold.

They proceeded into the parlor, making small talk while the cook put the final touches on their dinner. A short time later they were seated at the long dining room table, being served by the efficient butler. Niall had been here many times for Sunday dinner, but today the pompous atmosphere and over-abundance of formality bothered him. Before, he'd taken it as a sign of what to expect, and had tried to accustom himself to her life style. Today he winced at the display of such wealth and pretense.

"Papa, look! The duck still has a head." Beth pointed to the large bird being placed on the table. She was kneeling on her chair, leaning into the table, and staring at the bird's eyes.

"Do not point, Beth, it shows poor manners. And sit down," Jocelyn corrected in a stern tone.

She would not put up with the girl's dreadful behavior today.

Niall didn't like Jocelyn's tone. "I'll take care of this," his pointed words were directed at their hostess. He looked at his daughter. "Jocelyn's right, Beth. You need to sit down and we'll talk about the duck while we eat." He did agree with Beth about the bird.

"Niall, I don't think it appropriate to discuss the meal with a six year old..." Jocelyn began.

"But I'm seven, Papa," Beth protested.

"Beth, do not interrupt me when I am speaking." Turning to Niall, "Don't you think you need to discipline her? Perhaps she shouldn't be allowed at this table. She should be eating in the kitchen with the help." Jocelyn was beginning to lose her composure.

Niall cast a stern look at her. "That's enough, Jocelyn. I'll handle my daughter, and she will not eat in the kitchen. Not now, or ever." His voice was severe as he controlled his anger, as well as his desire to grab Beth and leave.

Jocelyn startled at his terse words, but said nothing.

"Beth, honey, let's eat. We can discuss the duck all you want on the way home. All right?"

"All right, Papa." Beth dropped her head to stare at her plate.

Dinner proceeded without further outbursts by either female, for which Niall was grateful. His appetite had soured, but he ate, sipped wine, and conversed with Jocelyn, but only to the extent necessary to be civil. The entire time he knew this wasn't where he wanted to be. Not in this house and not with this woman. His mind had been made up days ago, when he realized the true extent of his feelings for Kate. He just wanted to finish the meal and get out.

"Our dessert will be served in the parlor. Perhaps my maid can take Beth to the park while we talk?" Jocelyn wanted the child out of her house.

Niall thought Jocelyn's idea perfect. He'd be able to break it off with her today, in private. "How does that sound, Beth? Going to the park?" Niall leaned down to brush some crumbs from his daughter's cheek and watched a smile form on her lips.

"Yes, Papa. That would be fun."

A few minutes later the adults were alone. An awkward silence enveloped the room, but Jocelyn was nothing if not a good hostess, schooled in small talk. She was determined to salvage the afternoon.

"How is the ranch? Anything new?"

"The ranch is fine. Kate and Trent are moving the last of her belongings to their ranch today, so everything will be back to normal." Niall realized the house had seemed normal with Kate in it. Now it would feel empty.

"Good. It has been completely inappropriate to have a young, single woman living in the same house as three men. The gossip has been terrible. I'm surprised your family encouraged her to stay. Why, until her father arrived, she was the main topic for the town women, who spoke of her in all nature of foul terms. You should have heard them. Their comments were painful, but knowing their

169

words might be true was worse. Of course, I protested their accusations about her being nothing more than a strumpet, but their comments affected me, as it's common knowledge we plan to marry. But, I'm afraid the damage to Miss Garner's reputation is irreversible." Jocelyn's tone was full of scorn and disgust for Kate, as well as censure for the part the MacLarens had played in the arrangement. She had no idea he'd match her words of contempt with strong ones of his own.

"Her reputation?" His words were quiet, too quiet for the raging anger that had built in him as Jocelyn had continued her tirade. "And just what are you implying, Jocelyn?" Hardened eyes bored into hers as he advanced within a few feet of where she stood. "It's hardly a home of all men. Everyone knows Aunt Alicia and Beth are in the house. If the town believes my aunt would allow anything unseemly to happen in her house they are greatly mistaken. And you are mistaken to think I believe you played no part in these conversations. I'm no fool and understand the games you play better than you realize. Frankly, none of the MacLarens care what the gossips invent or say." In four long strides Niall was at the small bar. He grabbed a bottle from the shelf above and poured a generous amount of amber liquid into a glass. With one swallow he emptied it and poured another. He'd just lifted it to his lips when he was interrupted.

"Do you intend to drink the entire bottle?" Jocelyn huffed. How dare he use that tone with her. His words had shaken her, but she stood her ground, determined not to let this backwoods cowboy intimidate her. She was a van Deelin, far above anyone else in this dusty settlement.

He glanced at the glass in his hand, downed it and poured another. He considered the glass for a moment before the drink shot down his throat, warming him, and replacing his anger with a certainty of what would come next.

"What I intend to do and don't intend to do is none of your business. My life, and that of my family, is not open for discussion———least of all with you. We discussed how our lives would work *if* we ever married. My life would be mine."

"But wouldn't I have rights also, such as with Beth? Surely you don't expect me to mother your child without the ability to correct her mistakes and guide her upbringing?" Jocelyn was incredulous.

"That's exactly what I'd have expected. I wouldn't have expected you to mother Beth at all. You've never shown the least interest in Beth, or any child. Why would you believe I'd allow you to have a say in how I raise my daughter?"

"Because we will be married, and that's how it's done." Jocelyn felt the conversation spiral out of her control.

Niall let his temper calm before answering in a level voice. "No, Jocelyn, we won't be getting married. It has become quite clear to me that a marriage between us, even one of mutual convenience, is out of the question."

"But our plans, think of what you would be tossing aside."

"Believe me, I am thinking of everything I would throw away if you and I did marry." In his mind he pictured Kate. Her laugh, quick smile, honesty, and kind nature were a complete contrast to the woman standing before him. "I'm also thinking of how a marriage to you would affect the lives of my family. I now believe it would cause tremendous discontent and be the greatest mistake of my life." He set his glass on the table and started toward the foyer.

"Niall, wait, please." Jocelyn followed him but already knew it was too late. The man had made his decision.

"No, Jocelyn. I'm sorry, but I'm no longer interested in the future we discussed. I'll be seeing you around Fire Mountain, but will no longer call on you." He tipped his hat and walked out the door.

"It's the girl, isn't it? You're sleeping with her, just like your saloon whore, aren't you?" Jocelyn spat out to his retreating back, her venomous hatred of Kate now undisguised.

Niall stopped dead. He turned and walked back up the steps to stand in front of her.

"This decision is mine, for my own reasons. Whether Kate enters into it or not is none of your concern. And understand this. If I hear one negative word about Kate, or about Miss Chalmette, I'll consider you the source. Do not cross me, Jocelyn. I'm not someone you want for an enemy." His jaw worked but he said nothing more.

Jocelyn watched him go, stunned he'd spurned her for a girl of no standing, with no money, and a tainted reputation.

Chapter Twenty-Two

The days seemed to fly after their move. Trent had approached Niall about a purchase he wanted to make. The two had negotiated a price, and Kate was now the proud owner of Captain. She was thrilled. Alicia told her the family wanted her to stay as Beth's governess, if she still wanted the position, and the schedule could adjust to accommodate her duties at her new home. Kate saw no reason to change Beth's routine. She planned to do her chores early, then ride over to the MacLaren's, work with Beth in the morning, and ride back to her father's ranch each afternoon. She hoped this schedule would allow her little time to encounter Niall.

Kate still felt the excitement of being able to live at her father's ranch—their ranch, as her father called it. He was clear he'd bought it for both of them, and if anything happened to him, it would pass to Kate. It was a good feeling, knowing she had security, but she didn't want to discuss it further as she had no intention of letting her father go anytime in the foreseeable future. He'd just have to stay healthy and be safe, and Kate had told him as much.

"Afternoon, Kate. Did you have a good day at the MacLaren's?" Josh threw over his shoulder as he moved hay from the barn to the adjacent corral.

"Hello, Josh. Yes, a wonderful day. Beth is so bright it's a joy to teach her. Where's Father?"

"Niall and Jamie stopped by earlier. The boss was needed for a meeting in town. Said not to wait supper for him." Josh stopped long enough to wipe his brow. "Oh, yes. Niall asked about you."

"Thanks." Kate was surprised Niall had mentioned her at all. "Well, then, would you like to take supper in the house with me tonight? You haven't joined us in a while, and I'd love the company." Kate liked Josh, his smile, and personality. She'd heard of his way with women, but Kate knew she'd never fall for a man like him. Someone who seemed to have no interest in ever settling down with one woman. No, she simply sought the company of someone who could make her laugh, relax. Just for an evening.

"That sounds good. Call when you're ready for me." Josh smiled at the invitation. It was always good to share dinner with a beautiful woman, especially one like Kate. She was out of his reach, though. He'd seen the looks passing between Niall and Kate, and until Niall finalized his plans to marry the van Deelin woman, Josh would keep his interest to himself.

******

"Doc, Sam." Trent, acknowledged the men already at the table when he, Jamie, and Niall arrived. "Is Sheriff Rawlins going to make it?"

"No. Had to ride down to Phoenix, but Hen and Jerrod should be here any minute." Sam looked over to see the two men walk through the door.

They'd gathered to discuss the robberies and the young thieves involved. What Trent had learned from Tommy surprised and angered him. The boy's father had taken off with some woman he'd met

174

during their journey from Missouri, abandoning his family to their own fate. They'd been headed to a small town in California where his wife, Joanne Babbett, had kin.

Mrs. Babbett had decided it was best to keep going as there weren't enough provisions to make it back to Missouri. Besides, there was no place to go back to. Her husband had sold everything and took off with most of the money when he abandoned them.

"What kind of man does that to his wife and kids?" Trent asked, almost to himself, after he'd filled the others in on what he'd learned. The others could only shake their heads in disgust.

The men ordered drinks and food before Jerrod Minton, the local attorney, spoke up. "You all know the sheriff decided to keep the girl at the jail until he can find the mother. The boy hasn't given us any more information since Trent got him to talk over a week ago. Won't show us her location. Doesn't trust lawmen, at least that's what Rawlins said. Gloria's bringing food to her at the jail and sending some back with Tommy when he stops by, but we need to decide what we're going to do about this situation."

Doc Minton, Jerrod's father, wiped his mouth and placed the napkin back in his lap. "Well, I do have news. Tommy came to the clinic late yesterday. Begged me to follow him to check out his Ma. She's not good, a small fever, but I believe she'll pull through. Needs care and food, but refuses to leave the shack. I don't think she has any idea what her children have done."

Doc stopped long enough to sip his coffee, add some sugar, then try another sip, all the while gauging the reactions of his friends. Apparently satisfied with the coffee as well as the effect his words had on the men at the table, he continued. "Alma had her convinced she and Tommy both had jobs in town. That's how they're buying food. According to Mrs. Babbett, the Ma, Alma's fourteen and Tommy's ten. I didn't ask about the jewelry, but Mrs. Babbett says Alma's been going to the mercantile for supplies. That right, Hen?"

"That's right, basic stuff like bread, jam, eggs, milk, never any candy or other items you'd expect kids to buy. I didn't place her at first when I saw her in the jail as she always wore a dress into the store and had her hair in a bonnet. I didn't connect the two until right now," Hen said.

"So we have a sick woman, a boy that's too young to get a job that would pay for their keep, and a daughter who was caught stealing but lying to her Ma about it. That about sum it up?" Niall asked no one in particular. The others nodded, each trying to come up with an idea on how to settle this mess for both the victims and the woman with two kids.

"Boy says his Ma is a real good cook. Says Alma's great with horses. Guess they used to raise them in Missouri. Maybe we can find someone looking for a cook, and kids who aren't afraid to work," Doc said.

Trent leaned forward, placing his arms on the table. "Normally, I'd say that's a good idea, Doc. But who's going to want to take in a couple of kids who are known thieves? And who haven't made any effort to return the property, or even admit they're guilty? Those are a couple of sizable hurdles in my opinion."

Sam downed the remainder of his coffee, motioning the waitress to refill his cup. "You know, Trent's made an excellent point. First thing we need to do is confront Alma with what we know, and that we're going to bring her Ma in for questioning. Scare her enough to get her to confess. Once that's done, she'll talk about the jewelry. My gut tells me it's desperation and circumstances making them steal, nothing more."

"So, we at least hope to find the jewelry and return it." Niall summed up what they were all thinking. "I doubt much of the cash is still around, but returning the jewelry may be enough once people understand their situation. What do we do about the family at that point?"

"Get Mrs. Babbett well and find them some work, at least until they're ready to move on. Someone always needs a good cook, and the girl's strong enough to help at one of the ranches. Put the word out once the jewelry's been returned. See what happens," Jerrod said. He pushed back his chair and stood. "I need to get back to the office, but I'll do whatever I can to help. You know that. Fire Mountain's a generous town. I've no doubt it'll work out for this family, the same as it has for the rest of us." He nodded to the other men as he turned to leave.

******

"You know, Niall, you didn't need to ride all the way back to the ranch with me. I could've found it on my own." Trent chuckled at the look of discomfort on Niall's face. "Or is there something else on your mind?"

"Well, yes, there is. Thought maybe I'd say hello to Kate, if she's here." Niall had missed Kate not living at the ranch, being able to see her a few days a week. Now she rode over just long enough to teach Beth and visit with Alicia. She'd ride back to the Garner place before he'd finished his work each day. Niall had seen her a few times since he'd called it off with Jocelyn, but not long enough to have a real conversation, let Kate know where things stood with him.

"Lights are on, so I believe she must be here. Come on in," Trent said, but stopped when he heard laughter coming from inside. Stepping through the front door he saw Kate, on her hands and knees, with Josh next to her, his hand on her back. "Evening, Josh. What's going on here?"

"Hey, Boss," Josh said and immediately removed his hand.

"Evening, Papa. How was your time in town?" Kate asked the question without taking her eyes from the floor.

"Will someone tell me what's going on?" Trent had become more curious as the two moved around the floor on their hands and knees.

"Oh, nothing much. I was showing Josh the necklace I made for Beth and the strand broke. Everything went flying." Kate laughed and Josh joined her. "Landed in Josh's dinner, over the table, on the floor––everywhere." She laughed harder, and reached over to place a hand on Josh's arm. "One landed right in his spoon as he was taking a bite."

"Sure was a sight." Josh smiled at her and noticed she hadn't removed her hand from his arm.

They both sat back on their haunches and noticed the second man in the room.

Niall. Kate's stomach tightened and her heart picked up a few beats.

"Hello, Kate. Josh," Niall said, never taking his eyes from the woman on the floor. *So I may have waited too long.*

"Niall. Good to see you, again." Josh stumbled over the words, understanding the impression this little scene made. "Well, unless you need some more help, Kate, I guess I'll be going. Thanks for dinner." He grabbed his hat and headed for the door. "Boss. Niall. See you both later."

Niall's eyes continued to stare at the retreating form, but Trent turned to Kate, who was now clearing away the supper dishes.

"So you had Josh over for dinner, I take it?" Her father eyed her, wondering why she'd asked their foreman over while he was away.

"Yes. You were in town, Josh had no plans, and I felt like company. Anyway, he enjoys my chicken and biscuits, and there was plenty," Kate said as she continued to clean the table.

"Uh-huh," Trent responded.

"What does that mean?" Kate glared at her father for a second before she decided to ignore him, and their guest.

179

"Nothing, Kate. Niall stopped by to speak with you, if you have a few minutes."

"That's okay. Another time might be better," Niall said. "Thanks for riding with us to the meeting. I'll talk with Aunt Alicia about a cook, but doubt we've a need right now. Someone will come forward, I'm sure of it." Niall nodded to Kate, who'd stopped what she was doing to listen to their conversation. "Nice to see you." With nothing more to say, he turned and walked out the door.

"I thought he wanted to speak with me?" Kate cast her father a confused look when the door slammed shut.

"Well, he did. Guess the spectacle of you on your hands and knees with Josh sort of changed his mind," Trent said, his voice a little more curt than he intended.

Kate ran out the door. "Niall. Niall, wait!" she called as he passed the barn. He stopped Zeus, turned to glance over his shoulder, and reined his horse around to where Kate stood.

"What is it, Kate?"

"Father said you came by to speak with me. Hmm..." She paused to moisten her lips. "Do you still want to talk?" Kate was more hopeful than she should be. The odds were he wanted to talk about Beth, or his aunt. But she still held her breath.

"It can wait. It's late, I'm tired, and I still have to ride back to the ranch." What he wanted was to jump off Zeus, wrap his arms around her, and tell her she was his. Not Josh's. Not anyone else's. Only his.

"Well, if you're sure. You're welcome to come in for coffee if you want. I'm sure father would welcome the company."

But not you, he thought. "Thanks, but another time would be better. Good night, Kate."

"Good night, Niall." She walked back to the house feeling a large hole open in her heart.

Chapter Twenty-Three

It was a Saturday night when Kate first realized she was late. Her monthly courses were never late. Never. But, as she lay in bed and tried to calm her rising panic, she told herself there had been a lot happening, which she heard could have an impact on her timing. She was two weeks late—not much, she reasoned. She expected it would start tomorrow in church, because, well, that's the way things happened.

But it didn't happen at church, nor did it start the following week, or the next. By then Kate was nauseous part of each day and doing anything she could to hide it from everyone. Her clothes were getting a little tight, but not so much that anyone else would notice.

Kate felt utterly alone. Niall hadn't tried to speak with her again the few times they'd seen each other at the ranch. He hadn't announced plans with Jocelyn, but Kate still assumed it was simply a matter of time. She'd never be able to approach him. She couldn't say anything to her father as his disappointment in her would be more than she could bear. Plus, he'd insist she tell him who the father was. No, speaking with her father wasn't an option. She couldn't confide in Alicia, either. There were no real friends she could count on in town, except perhaps one. Doc Minton. She needed to confirm one way or the other, and the one person to see was the Doc. Friday—if she hadn't started by then, she'd ride to town and meet with the doctor.

Kate didn't start by Friday, and it wasn't Doc Minton who was at the clinic. It was Caleb. Of all the awful situations. Doc Minton was in Phoenix and wouldn't be back for a week. Well, she could swallow her pride and see Caleb or wait another week—another week of not knowing.

Caleb stood in the clinic entry with a warm greeting, asking what she needed. But Kate just gazed up at the man who'd shared her fate in the stagecoach accident, then stared past him to the open clinic door, nausea creeping up on her at the realization of what she must admit.

"Kate?"

"Oh, sorry, Doctor McCauley," Kate said, but the doctor cut her short.

"Caleb, Kate. I think you and I can be informal, don't you?" His voice calmed her.

"Caleb, then." She nodded to him as he moved to the side so she could pass into the office. This was humiliating. What would he think of her? Would he feel compelled to tell her father? Or worse, ask about the baby's father?

"Are you going to tell me why you're here, Kate? There must be some reason that brought you to the clinic." Caleb's voice was quiet, soothing her jangled nerves.

"I...I just don't know where else to go for this," she said, and the tears started to flow.

Caleb looked at her for a minute, then ushered her into the exam room in the back. He sat her down on one chair while he took the other.

"Why don't you tell me what's going on and we'll go from there, all right? Whatever it is, there will be a solution."

She swallowed, trying to clear her jumbled thoughts and let her tears dry. She never cried, but now she couldn't seem to get control. Kate couldn't bring herself to look Caleb in the eye. Her throat worked, but the words wouldn't come.

"Kate, look at me." Her head came up as she tried to focus on Caleb. "That's it. A little more so we can see each other while we talk." She followed his instructions and took a ragged breath as his eyes met hers.

"Oh Caleb, I'm so stupid," Kate started.

"Well, you may be many things Kate, but I have yet to see you do anything stupid."

She glanced away, gathered her courage, and plunged ahead.

"I need you to tell me if I'm pregnant."

An audible whoosh of air escaped Caleb's lips before he recovered. "I see. Well, let's start with the basics. How long since your last monthly?"

"Over nine weeks."

"Are you pretty regular?"

Kate nodded. "Yes. Very."

"Nauseous, vomiting?"

"Yes. Off and on for the last few weeks. But then I feel fine the rest of the day."

"All right, Kate. I'll need to do an exam to be sure, so why don't you get ready while I step outside. Holler when you're ready." Caleb could feel the misery rolling off Kate in waves. Of anything she could have told him, this was the last thing he would have suspected, but it was imperative Caleb not let Kate sense his thoughts. He didn't want his reaction adding to her distress.

Thirty minutes later Kate was sitting in his office, listening as Caleb confirmed what she already knew in her heart. Yes, she was pregnant. Based on the date she had given him, the baby would be close to eight weeks along. There wasn't much to do about the sickness. It would subside soon and she'd feel better.

"Does the father know?" It was a standard question, but somehow asking it of Kate was harder than with other patients.

"No, Caleb. You're the only one I've told. I don't want anyone else to know about my situation."

"Kate, you have to understand that the idea of keeping this concealed is unreasonable. You live on the ranch with your father. You work for the MacLarens. You attend church and shop in town. Unless you move from the area, it will be impossible to keep it a secret after the next couple of weeks. Is that what you want? To move until the baby is born?"

Kate was miserable. "I don't know what I want, except telling the father is impossible. He has plans to marry someone he's been seeing for months. This will ruin all his plans."

"But, Kate, what about his responsibility to the baby? Maybe he'd want to know, want to wed you, and give the baby his name. Have you thought about it from his side?" Caleb was being reasonable, trying to talk it through with her and offer opinions. It wasn't what she'd expected, but it was what she needed.

"No, he wouldn't want my baby, Caleb," she said, remembering Niall telling her he'd never be able to love her, and he sought marriage for the sole purpose of furthering his ambitions. The tears started again and ran down her cheeks. She brushed them away, took another breath, and stared at nothing in particular.

"Kate, the Niall I have come to know would want to take full responsibility."

Her head snapped up at this. She hadn't mentioned Niall to Caleb, yet he knew. "How do you know the father is Niall, or what he'd want?" Kate's voice had risen with a hint of desperation.

"For three reasons. One, he broke it off with Jocelyn. It's not common knowledge, but he mentioned it to me a couple of weeks ago. Two, I see the way he is with Beth. He's a caring person and loves his daughter, his family. Niall wouldn't let a child grow up without a father if he had a way to stop it. And three, the man's in love with you."

"Loves me? Now I know you don't understand Niall. He keeps me around because of Beth, but he holds no affection for me. Love is out of the question." Kate wished with everything she had that what Caleb said was true, but she knew it wasn't.

"Do you want to hear how I know he loves you?"

Kate nodded.

"He told me."

Kate was incredulous. "What? Niall told you that?" She knew he didn't love her, but why would Caleb say it if he didn't think it was true.

"Niall and I had dinner a couple of weeks ago, at Mattie's. It was the same night he told me about Jocelyn. We had a few drinks during dinner, and afterwards we sat in Mattie's bar and had a couple more. By then he was pretty relaxed, and began to talk."

Kate looked up, startled, and began to say something, when Caleb raised his hand to stop her.

"No one else heard our conversation. It was private, and trust me, he wasn't drunk. He told me he'd made the biggest mistake of his life, and was trying to figure out how to fix it. He told me he'd done something that resulted in hurting someone he'd grown to love. He mentioned she lived at a nearby ranch. He never mentioned your name, but it didn't take much to figure out he was speaking of you."

Kate sat stone still, absorbing Caleb's words.

"You need to think about telling him, Kate. He may surprise you."

Chapter Twenty-Four

Kate had left Captain at the livery and walked to the clinic. When she left her meeting with Caleb, all she could think about was that she was pregnant—pregnant with Niall's baby—a baby he wouldn't want and probably wouldn't acknowledge. No matter what Caleb thought, Niall didn't love her. Even if he had stopped seeing Jocelyn, he'd made his feelings quite clear. She'd raise the baby alone rather than be tied to a man who could never love her.

"I will never be able to love you." Niall's words came back to her in a rush as she headed toward the livery on the wooden walkway. The words haunted her, and no matter how hard she tried, she couldn't push them from her mind. She was certain he'd been sincere.

But what if what Caleb said was true? Could she mean more to Niall than he let on? Was that what he'd wanted to speak with her about when he stopped by the house a few weeks ago? Should she consider telling him and risk the further humiliation of his rejection? Too many questions. Kate needed time to think.

She wrapped her coat tight around her to ward off the cold night air. If she could sit somewhere and concentrate, the answers might come. She needed to focus on what to do next. Mattie's was down the street with its well-lit interior, fireplace, and Mattie's own homemade pie. Kate decided she'd

188

stop for pie and a cup of hot coffee, sit a while, and sort out her options, which she knew were few.

A short time later she felt better. Caleb was right. She could either leave town to have the baby, or stay and confront Niall. Leaving wasn't an option, so she'd have to gather her courage and speak with the baby's father. But whatever his response, she would keep her baby.

Maybe Caleb was right about the rest of it, too. She and Niall had spoken just a few times, but when they did, she was the one who'd been curt, and he was the one trying to build a bridge. Kate had refused his attempts. She believed he'd been honest with her that night, but what if his feelings for her had changed? Perhaps if she approached him, he'd surprise her, as Caleb had said.

Caleb wasn't the first to mention that Niall had stopped courting Jocelyn. Alicia and her father had both told her he now took Sunday dinners at home and hadn't mentioned the woman's name in weeks, but Kate had refused to believe either of them. She didn't dare hope, finding it easier to plan a life without him.

Kate decided she had little to lose and much to gain by being honest with Niall. If he cared about her at all, and learned of their unborn child, she knew he'd offer marriage. Perhaps he'd come to love them both. If not, well, she wasn't any worse off than she was now, but at least she'd have her answer. She would have Niall's baby even if she couldn't have him.

She started to grab her coat when the door swung open and an extremely attractive woman, whom Kate had never seen before, entered. When she removed her coat, Kate could see she wore a striking blue gown, cut somewhat lower in the front than normal, but still acceptable, and a beautiful silver necklace with blue stones. Her hair was a rich brown, and as she turned toward the dining room, Kate could see she had warm golden-brown eyes.

But the next sight startled Kate into sitting back down. Niall followed the woman into the dining room. Kate's breath caught. He was the most handsome man she'd ever seen, in black slacks that fit him well, black jacket, a white shirt with black ribbon tie, and a blue brocade vest that matched the woman's dress.

He took the coat from the woman and hung it along with his overcoat on a stand near the entrance. As they turned to be shown to their table Kate saw Niall rest his hand on the small of the woman's back in a gesture that was both intimate and familiar. It was obvious this was someone Niall knew very well.

He laughed at something the woman said as he pulled out her chair. After she was seated, Niall moved around the table. That's when he saw Kate, sitting alone in the corner. He stopped cold and stared at her.

Kate was the last person he'd thought to see on an early Friday evening in Mattie's. But here she sat, her back rigid, her eyes steady on his, and her hands folded in her lap. She was working the gold ring, twisting it between her thumb and index finger, a gesture he recognized from her weeks at the ranch. Only now she wore the ring on her right hand, not the left. Her light blonde hair was coming loose from the bun and strands were streaming down her neck to cover the black coat she had bundled around her.

It was a moment before her eyes wavered from his. She stood, grabbing her small bag before walking straight toward him, or rather, straight for the door.

"Kate, wait." Niall moved behind Kate and placed a hand on her arm. She turned to look up at him but said nothing.

"Kate, I can explain why I'm here tonight." The comment surprised him. He didn't have to explain himself to Kate or anyone. But Niall had felt guilt when their eyes met, guilt about treating Gloria to a night out when the woman he loved sat alone, dejected.

"You owe me nothing, Mr. MacLaren, least of all an explanation of how you spend your evenings. After all, I'm just your employee." Her words were thick and forced. She wanted to leave, but his hand was still on her arm.

"You are not just an employee, Kate." Niall sounded pained, as if her words had hurt him somehow.

"Well, someone of no consequence then." Kate glanced around him to the woman, then back to Niall. "You have a beautiful lady waiting for you. I suggest you get on with your evening, and let me get on with mine."

Niall held her arm a moment longer while gazing into her too-bright eyes. He didn't want her to go but couldn't make her stay.

"All right, Kate." He released her.

Kate walked out the door toward the livery, without a backward glance.

******

"Who was that, Niall?" Gloria never pried, but she had her suspicions.

"Katherine Garner," Niall said.

"Ah, the houseguest. She didn't seem well. Do you think she needs help getting home? It's getting dark and appears rain might be coming."

"I'm sure she's not in town alone. Besides, she wouldn't let me help her anyway. She has no use for me. It's your birthday, Gloria, and I always take you out on your birthday. We never missed one, even when Camille was alive. I'm not about to change our plans because of Miss Garner." But even as he spoke Niall peered through the outside window for a last glance, just to be sure she was okay, at least that's what he told himself, but Kate was already out of sight.

"All right, if you're sure, but I think it's a mistake." Most people in town knew Gloria was a generous woman, and many overlooked her profession because of it. Gloria was always watching out for those in trouble and those needing a hand up.

They had begun their supper when Caleb walked into Mattie's. He'd finished up at the clinic and needed a drink as well as a hot meal.

Niall offered his hand and then pointed to an empty chair. "Join us, Caleb."

"Good evening, Miss Chalmette. You look stunning tonight." Caleb did appreciate a beautiful woman and Gloria was that.

"Why thank you, Caleb. I've asked you to call me Gloria. It's my birthday and Niall was generous enough to ask me to supper. Please join us." The smile she gave Caleb was luminous, bringing a smile to his face.

"Well, I don't know how to refuse an offer to help celebrate your birthday, Gloria. Thank you." Caleb was exhausted and still haunted by the conversation with Kate. The last thing he expected was to find Niall with Gloria at Mattie's. He was glad Kate hadn't seen them.

"Long day, Doc?" Niall asked after Caleb had ordered a drink and dinner.

"Very. Ended a little while ago, but the last patient was more challenging than most, and I've spent the last hour trying to figure out the next steps." He wouldn't reveal anything, but was glad to get at least that much off his chest.

"Reminds me, Caleb," Gloria said, "Miss Garner was in the restaurant when we arrived and she didn't seem at all well. She appeared pale and stressed, and left as soon as we arrived. I thought maybe you could find time to check on her. I've seen a lot of girls on the edge, and she had that look."

Caleb glanced at Niall and saw what he expected—guilt. In Caleb's experience it was never good for a woman you love to see you with another beautiful woman on a night out, no matter what the reason.

"Kate was here? How long ago did she leave?" Worry etched Caleb's face. He knew she was on Captain, over two months pregnant, and had a good forty-minute ride back to the ranch, and that was if the weather held.

"Twenty or thirty minutes ago. Why?" Niall became concerned by what he saw on his friend's face.

"Because I did speak with her earlier, and know she rode her horse to town. Alone. Truth is, she wasn't feeling well. Last thing she needs is to get caught in this weather, not to mention run into whoever might be out on the trail at this time of night. I better grab the buggy and go after her." Caleb started to stand but Niall restrained him.

"I'll go, Doc. It'll be faster if I take Zeus. You stay here with Gloria, if it's all right with you?" He looked to the woman who was his guest.

"Of course, Niall, you go. We'll finish this another time."

That was all the encouragement he needed. Niall was out the door the next minute, heading for the livery and Kate.

******

"We're just a little ways from the ranch, Captain," Kate said to her horse as they worked their way through the cold down pour. She was coughing, and chilled clear through. It had been much warmer when she left the ranch, but now sleet was forming. Her basic coat provided little protection. She regretted her decision not to get a room in town.

194

She felt dizzy and thought of holing up under a stand of trees, but rejected the idea as soon as she had it. She'd only become more chilled, and would still need to get home. No, she needed to continue to the ranch as fast as possible.

A few minutes later a stiff wind sprang up. The sleet fell harder, gusting into them and pushing Captain to the edge of the path. A burst of lightning caused Captain to startle. Kate's reaction was swift. She brought him under control, urging him on. A few minutes later another bolt hit the ground not a hundred feet away, startling Captain into a series of bucks that threw Kate off and into a large group of bushes. She landed hard, but didn't think she was hurt. She thought of the baby. Oh God, what now? Captain was out there, but she couldn't see or hear him in this weather. Violent shivers racked her body. She tried to stand, but collapsed. She must have broken or sprained her ankle. Her cough grew worse and the dizziness returned. She curled into a ball, wrapped the coat around her, and tried to burrow further under the thick branches. Kate decided to rest a little while, wait out the storm, and then walk to the ranch. *I'll be all right. The baby and I will both be all right,* was her last thought as her eyes rolled back and everything went black.

******

Where the hell is she? Trent was frantic. The weather continued to worsen, and there was still no sign of Katherine. According to Josh, she'd left hours before, riding into town on Captain. His foreman had been unsuccessful in his attempts to get her to wait until he could accompany her. Kate had refused. She had an appointment she couldn't miss.

"Boss, let me ride into town and find her. I'm sure she's okay, but we'll both rest easier when we know for sure." Josh felt miserable as well as responsible for Kate being out on a night like this, alone.

"No, Josh. Katherine's a smart gal. She would have enough sense to find a place in town to wait out the storm." At least that's what Trent prayed as he continued to gaze at the lightning storm through the front window.

******

Niall thought he heard hooves coming toward him, but couldn't see a thing in this storm. It had hit fast and hard just as he'd left town. Only one trail led toward the turnoff to the Garner ranch, and Zeus was fast. He was certain he'd catch up to her soon.

Niall wore his greatcoat over the warm wool dress coat he had taken to dinner. He wasn't cold or uncomfortable, but was pretty sure Kate had nothing more than the coat she was wearing when she left the restaurant. He heard hooves again and this time saw the horse running towards him. *Captain. God, no.* Where was Kate? Fear gripped him. Had her horse spooked and thrown her? He had to find her and get her to the ranch before this storm got any worse. He rode forward, grabbed Captain's reins while turning the horse back around, then rode on, keeping his eyes focused, and scanning the trail.

Ten minutes later Captain whinnied, shook his head, then pulled forward toward some brush just off the trail. Niall scanned the area but couldn't see anything in the darkness. The wind had stilled somewhat and rain now fell in soft drops instead of the earlier driving pellets. Captain continued forward and began to nudge something. Niall couldn't see what the horse was after. He sat astride Zeus another minute until he heard what sounded like a soft moan. Jumping from his horse he was at the bushes in three long strides, pulling back the branches and peering beneath to find Kate. *Oh, please, not Kate, too.*

She was curled in a ball, her clothes soaked through. Her small frame was consumed with uncontrollable shivers as her body tried in vain to keep her warm. Niall worked fast, checking for broken bones. He whistled to Zeus, lifted Kate, and mounted his horse, installing Kate across his lap. Pulling first his wool coat, then his greatcoat, around both of them, he urged Zeus forward. He estimated about twenty minutes to the Garner spread, but just another ten to his. He turned toward home.

Chapter Twenty-Five

"Aunt Alicia, Jamie, Drew, Will." Niall carried Kate into the house and up the stairs. "I need help. Now!" Alicia and Drew came running.

"My God, Niall, is that Kate?" Drew was the first to reach them as Niall walked into Kate's old room and placed her gently on the bed.

"What is it, Niall?" Alicia asked as she entered the bedroom and dashed to the bed. She took one look at the situation and began ordering Niall and Drew to bring blankets, warm water, and warm clothes. She hurried to pull the wet garments from Kate's shaking body, then dried her with towels Niall had thrown on the bed before grabbing blankets. What Alicia saw didn't surprise her, as it would have someone else. The conversation she'd overheard several weeks ago confirmed what she'd suspected for some time. The slight roundness of Kate's belly gave it all away. Alicia moved directly, but discreetly, between Niall and Kate, obstructing any view he might have had. "Niall, we need Doc Minton, and someone should go after Trent." Alicia looked at her nephew with concerned eyes.

"Will she be okay?" Niall's voice was small, almost a whisper, and his worry was evident.

"I don't know. She needs the doctor," Alicia said.

Niall turned to Drew who nodded, headed down the stairs to find Will, and alert Gus and Pete.

"I'll head to town. Pete, you go get Trent," Gus yelled. "Drew, you and Will should stay here in case Niall needs anything."

Within minutes both men were mounted, with Pete riding toward the Garner ranch and Gus to town. Drew ran back into the house to find that Alicia had cleaned Kate up, applied salve to her scrapes, pulled warm clothes over her shaking body, and covered her with several blankets. Niall had gone to the kitchen to warm some broth, and returned within minutes to set the bowl next to the bed.

"Do you want to tell us what happened?" Getting to this point had taken about fifteen minutes, but it seemed like an hour since Alicia had looked down at the young woman whom she'd grown to love—a young woman she now knew was carrying her nephew's child.

Niall changed into dry clothes and sat down on the edge of the bed. "I don't know for sure, but I saw her just before she left town. Then the storm hit. Something must've spooked Captain, and he bucked Kate off. The little fool had ridden to town in nothing but a light weight coat, and started home as the sun was setting."

"And you let her leave? What were you thinking, letting her ride off like that? My God, Niall, she could've been killed." Alicia was livid and overcome with worry.

"Don't you think I know that?" Niall tried to control the escalating panic he felt as well as the angry words to his aunt. He was failing at both. The first sight of Kate on the ground had turned his stomach to ice. Her eyes had been glazed and she'd been unable to stop the massive shivers that rolled over her body. He'd wanted to scream at God for letting this happen, but searching within himself, he knew the blame fell to him. He could've stopped her. He should've stopped her. Why did he keep making all the wrong decisions where Kate was concerned?

Both Alicia and Niall were saved from saying something each might regret when Caleb rushed into the room, Jamie close behind. Alicia moved aside as Caleb pulled the covers back. What he saw made him turn and ask everyone but Alicia to leave the room so he could tend to Kate. Niall was reluctant at first, but Drew put his arm around his older brother's shoulder, guiding him out of the room and down the stairs with Jamie following behind.

"Where's Kate?" Trent entered the house moments later, his eyes wild.

"Upstairs with the Doc," Niall said. Trent nodded and started for the stairs.

"Trent." Drew began to warn him of the doctor's instructions, but stopped at the worry he saw on the man's face.

Trent just glared at Drew as he took the stairs two at a time. He didn't knock, but threw open the bedroom door and hurried toward his daughter.

"Trent, it would be better if you let Alicia and I tend to Kate, alone. You can wait downstairs with the others." Caleb knew his words fell on deaf ears.

He threw the same *don't-mess-with-me* glare at the doctor he'd given Drew. "To hell with that, Doc. I'm staying with my daughter."

"All right, but you must move over to the other side and stay out of the way. I need to perform a complete examine on Kate. I'm warning you, Trent, do not interfere, or I'll have the boys come up and escort you down. We understand each other?"

Taken aback, Trent nodded his agreement and motioned with his hand for the doctor to get started.

Kate hadn't stirred since she was brought into the room. She moaned occasionally, but nothing more. Caleb was thorough, not ignoring anything that might indicate internal damage. When the doctor began to check the baby, Trent came off the wall, but was stilled with a harsh glare.

Caleb had just finished, and was pulling the covers back over Kate, when her eyes opened and she tried to speak.

"It's okay, Kate. You're safe. You don't need to talk now. Just rest and get warm." Caleb didn't want her agitated or trying to get up. Trent and Alicia both moved closer to the bed.

Kate wouldn't have any of it. "No, no," she whispered but couldn't finish. She tried twice more to speak before anxious words escaped her lips. "The baby? My baby, Caleb?"

Alicia closed her eyes and prayed that Trent would handle the news well.

"Baby? What the hell is she talking about?" Trent gripped Caleb's arm, but the doctor pulled free.

"Settle down, Trent. She doesn't need you upsetting her." Caleb tried to calm Trent without success.

"I want an answer Caleb, and I want it now. What baby?" Trent softened his voice but moved into Caleb's space. He wasn't backing down.

Caleb took a deep breath, turned his head to Kate, then back to Trent. "Kate's pregnant."

"Pregnant? But how? She's been here or at our ranch since she got to town. There hasn't been anyone..." Trent's words froze. His face turned a deep red and the muscles in his neck became more prominent. He stared at Alicia, daring her to deny what they both knew was true.

"Now, Trent, calm down. There's an explanation." Alicia moved to the door to try to warn Niall, but it was too late.

"There is an explanation, and I'm going to beat the shit out of it right now." With that, Trent headed down the stairs straight toward Niall.

"Trent, what's going...?" Niall stood up from his chair, but was stopped with a hard blow to his jaw. He fell back onto a table, knocked over a lamp, and broke what was left of it when he landed. He tried to rise but was pulled up by his collar to receive a second hard blow before being shoved against a wall. Seconds before a third blow could land in Niall's gut, Trent was pulled off by three sets of arms that came around him from behind. Drew, Jamie, and Pete had been on the porch when they heard the commotion. What they saw stunned all three. It took just seconds for them to respond, restrain Trent, and stop the beating.

"Have you gone crazy, Trent? You could've killed him." Jamie was the first to speak as he pulled Trent back and threw him onto a nearby chair.

"I just might kill that son of a bitch if he gets near me anytime soon," Trent spat back.

"No, Trent, you won't. You will not kill the father of your grandchild." Alicia walked right up to the distraught man who was leaning forward, with his arms on his knees and his head resting in both hands.

That got everyone's attention, including Niall's. He was on his feet, rubbing his jaw, staring at his old friend, trying to make sense of what had just happened.

"Grandchild?" Niall whispered. All eyes shifted from Trent to Niall, but not a word was said.

"She's pregnant, Niall. Over two months along. That's why she came to town to see me today." Caleb had entered the room unnoticed, and walked up to Niall to examine the lacerations on his friend's face.

"Is it yours, Niall?" Trent's words were accusing and filled with pain.

He didn't hesitate. "Yes, Trent, the baby's mine." Niall's eyes moved to the stairs. He wanted nothing more than to go to her, hold her, and tell her everything would be all right. He'd take care of her and the baby. Instead, he turned to Caleb. "The baby, Doc, the baby's okay, right? And Kate? She'll pull through?" The full impact of Kate's decision to leave town alone hit Niall full force.

"As far as I can tell, Niall, the baby's fine. Kate will be, too. But I, for one, don't envy you the next few weeks. It's going to take a lot of quick talking if you want to make things right." Caleb looked over at Trent and saw the light dawn in the older man's eyes.

"You will marry my daughter, Niall." Trent enunciated each word. "You understand what I'm saying?" Trent pushed up from the chair as if he wanted to resume the beating he hadn't been able to finish.

"Yes, sir, I hear you. You'll get no argument from me. Kate and I will marry as soon as she is able."

Chapter Twenty-Six

"No, absolutely not. I will not marry Niall MacLaren, not ever. Never." Kate was awake, dressed, and furious. While she'd been recuperating, both families had planned her wedding to Niall, complete with the date—next Saturday—and who would be invited.

"Katherine," her father said. "You're not thinking straight. You're single, pregnant, and the baby's father wants to marry you. I don't understand why you're so upset and stubborn."

"He does not want me or the baby. You and I both know he's doing it because of you, not because of any feelings for me. No, I'm not going to marry him." Kate had to calm down. Her head was beginning to ache. She didn't know if it was due to the recent fall, or the pressure from everyone to marry Niall. She loved him. Oh, how she loved him. But she wouldn't force him to marry her out of guilt or duty. No, she'd have the baby and move away. She'd settle somewhere and hide behind the story that her husband, the baby's father, had died.

"I think you're wrong, Kate. I've spent the last few days with Niall, and believe me, he's determined to marry you, not because he feels he must, but because he wants both of you. You didn't see him the night he found you. He was a mess. And he became more of a mess when I laid into him about you being pregnant." Trent wasn't going to tell Kate that Niall had admitted his love for her. That was something the two of them had to work out on their own.

"Laid into him? You fought with him? Is he hurt?" Kate's worry for Niall gave Trent hope.

"He's fine. A little bruised maybe, but nothing broken." To think that a couple of days ago he wanted to kill Niall, and today he was trying to convince Kate to marry him.

A soft knock on the door got their attention.

"Kate, may I speak with you?" Niall's voice was gentle, hesitant.

Kate looked at her father, and Trent saw panic in her eyes. But maybe there was something more. Was it hope?

"Come on in, Niall. Kate and I are finished, for now." Trent walked over to place a kiss on his daughter's cheek and whisper in her ear. "Think of what's right for the baby and hear him out. You owe him at least that much." He nodded at Niall, then shut the door behind him.

Niall stared at Kate, looking from her beautiful blonde hair to her stormy blue eyes and the stark expression that showed pain, hope, and fear. He was the cause of all of it. She lifted her eyes to meet his as her right hand moved to her stomach, providing a protective cover for her baby––their baby. She glared at him, but found it hard to focus on anger as the love she still felt overwhelmed her. Kate wanted so much for this man to love her and their child, but she knew the truth. Niall would do anything for her father, even marry someone he cared nothing about. Kate raised her chin as she shook off the doubt, more determined than ever to remember he didn't want her, didn't want them.

Niall stood less than six feet away, arms at his sides, his hands out and palms up. "I want to work this out, Kate. Tell me what I need to say to convince you how much I want you and our baby in my life?"

Kate couldn't think when he was this close. He'd always had this effect on her. Even with all that had passed between them, she knew she'd never love anyone else the way she loved Niall.

"I know I've messed everything up between us. Said things I didn't mean. Tried to push you away to follow plans I thought were important, with a woman that meant nothing to me. The way I treated you that night, in this bedroom, was unforgivable. I know that. But I'm asking anyway. Please forgive me, Kate. Marry me. Make a life here, with me and our baby."

Kate's heart was pounding so hard she was sure Niall could hear it. His bright green eyes were focused on her, unwavering, waiting for her response. When none came, he moved closer until he was within inches of her. He reached out and took her hands in his.

"Kate, look at me. Let me know what you're thinking."

Get control, Kate. You can't stand here and let him throw out a few kind words and start believing everything will work out. It won't. He doesn't love you, but he cares deeply for your father. It would be a marriage built on nothing but guilt and a sense of responsibility for the child he helped create. No love, no warmth. None of the things she desired from the man she loved.

"I can't marry you, Niall. I won't marry you." Kate was surprised she was able to get the words out. "Both of us know your feelings about love, your decision not to love again. And, we both know how strong, how tough you are. When you make a decision, you stick with it, except perhaps in matters of honor, and the baby is a matter of honor with you. I realize you feel responsible for the child, but that's not enough for me.

"We would only end up making each other miserable. You, because you have made it clear you don't love me and never will, and me because I would always know the marriage was out of a sense of loyalty to my father, and responsibility to the baby, not because of any feelings for me. No, Niall, I'm not interested." Kate took a deep, shuddering breath and stepped back from him, staring at the floor. She didn't want to risk looking in his eyes and was afraid of what she might see.

"You're wrong, Kate. So very wrong about how I feel, and what our baby means to me." Niall turned and walked away from her so he wouldn't be tempted to grab Kate and pull her to him. "I've wanted you from the time I first saw you, ran you down on the boardwalk in Phoenix. Your effect on me was immediate, intense. It frightened the hell out of me. But I was safe, my plans were safe, because I knew you were taking the stage to California."

He stopped, turned towards her, then glanced around the room as if trying to decide how to continue. Niall shoved his hands into his pockets before his eyes moved back up to hers. "After the accident, when I found you lying in the stage, the same intense attraction slammed into me. It's no secret I objected to Alicia bringing you to the ranch. I didn't want you here, making me feel things I thought had been left behind when Camille died. The attraction continued to grow each time I saw you. But, like you said, I had plans to marry someone else—someone I didn't love and never could love—a marriage of convenience for political connections that would have made me and everyone in my family miserable." He walked back towards her, taking his hands from his pockets to shove them through his hair, then clasping them behind his neck while taking a deep, calming breath before he continued.

"Oh, I wanted you, Kate, make no mistake about that. But you were married, or so we all thought. You wore that gold band that warned me away. I became more determined than ever to go forward with my decision to marry Jocelyn. I couldn't have you, but I wanted you, loved you." He took a couple more steps. He was again within inches of her. "I tried. I tried pushing you away, ignoring you, flaunting my Sunday suppers in your face to make sure you knew there was someone else, but it was useless. I was more captured by you each day. Then the dance." He hesitated to go on but had to get it all out. His voice lowered to a whisper. "I was going to ask Jocelyn to marry me that night, did you know that?"

Kate looked at him and shook her head. He was so close, too close. She found it hard to breathe. She wanted to reach out, touch him, and wrap her arms around his neck for one of his drugging kisses. Believe that what he said was true and everything would be all right.

"But every time I saw you, someone else had you in his arms, making you laugh, enjoying your company. One man in particular."

"Sam," Kate whispered.

"Yes, Sam," Niall said. "You were the most beautiful woman I'd ever seen having a wonderful time with other men, but not me. My plans to avoid you all night collapsed, and the next thing I knew I was standing beside you. Who would've thought one dance would push me over the edge?" His eyes had turned a dark green as he spoke. His words were sometimes a whisper, then came out with force as he related his feelings.

"I took Jocelyn to her house, but left for home without proposing. Thoughts of you consumed me. I needed to touch you, kiss you, make love to you, Kate. I knew my control was slipping away, but there seemed to be nothing I could do." He stopped as if not quite believing what he'd done that night.

"Niall..." Kate started to reach out to him, but Niall looked away.

"Kate, I'm so damn sorry about that night." He took her hand and began to stroke circles with his thumb. "Not because of the baby, never that, but because it was your first time and it should have been special. It should have been slow, without any regrets. Instead, I said things I didn't mean, trying with all I had to push you away and make up for my inability to stay away from you. You had exposed my complete weakness for you, and when it counted, I was powerless to stop the hold you had on me. Then to discover you were a virgin." He dropped her hands and turned away. He rubbed his face with both hands and took another deep breath.

Kate stayed silent, watching the emotions play off his face as he struggled with his thoughts.

"Do you know what that meant to me? To know that no man had ever loved you before? You were mine, but I was too stubborn to see it, to grab onto it with both hands and hold on. God, what a fool I was." This time he walked over to a chair near the fireplace and sat down. He was quiet for a long time, his elbows resting on his knees with his forehead cradled in his hands. He sat there for so long that Kate found the courage to say what she'd wanted to for some time.

"You acted like I meant nothing to you. That it was only one night of pleasure. You said you didn't love me, could never love me." Her voice broke on the last, and she sat down on the edge of the bed with her hands over her face.

Niall winced at the truth of her statements. He rose from the chair and walked over to kneel in front of her. He grabbed her hands and stared up at her.

"Yes, you were a night's pleasure Kate, but a pleasure I want every night of my life."

Kate searched his face for any signs that might betray him, but saw none. But her doubts still lingered. If what he said were true, then who was the woman he was with the night she saw him at Mattie's?

"The woman you were with at Mattie's. Who is she?"

Niall watched her and saw so many questions in her eyes.

"Gloria. Her name is Gloria Chalmette."

"But who is she to you?"

He didn't want to bring his lover into this conversation. He wouldn't see her again if Kate agreed to marry him. He hadn't been with her since before the dance, the night he'd been with Kate. Niall knew he had to be honest with Kate if he was to win her trust.

"I have known her for over ten years. She owns a saloon in town. It's where I go on Friday nights."

"So she's the woman you go to town to be with? To sleep with?" The last three few words were said in a soft whisper.

"Yes."

"She is very beautiful."

"Yes."

"Do you love her?"

"No. Not in the way you mean."

"I don't understand."

"Gloria has been a good friend. She was there before my marriage to Camille, and then after Camille died. I was never with her, never slept with her, while I was married. It was two years after my wife died before I went back to see Gloria. I've seen her ever since. Our relationship is built on friendship, not on commerce, if you understand what I mean." He hoped Kate caught his meaning because he sure as hell didn't want to explain it further.

Kate looked at him, then a light went off in her head. Her eyes brightened and he knew she understood.

"But you don't love her?"

"I love her like a friend, and we've given each other what was needed—respect, compassion, advice, companionship. But not the kind of love I have for you. I never sought that with Gloria."

"But you didn't seek it with me, either."

"No, I didn't."

Kate seemed to work at accepting his explanations and not question him further about Gloria. Her heart told her he was being honest, but at the same time she warned herself to be cautious.

"And it's over with Jocelyn?"

"Yes."

The room was quiet for several minutes before Niall broke the silence

"Kate, look at me."

She lifted her head to gaze into eyes that had haunted her sleep for weeks. Eyes she wanted to look into for the rest of her life.

"I love you Kate, only you. Marry me, please."

That's when the tears came. They streamed down her face as he put his arms around her and drew her to him. He stroked her hair and drew lazy circles on her back as her sobs grew more intense, then began to subside. When the worst was over, Niall put a hand under her chin and raised her face to his so he could look into to her clear, blue eyes.

"Do you love me, Kate?"

More than you'll ever understand, Kate thought as she nodded. Niall's smile was instantaneous.

"Marry me." It was a whispered plea this time.

And the words he needed finally came. "Yes, Niall, I'll marry you."

Chapter Twenty-Seven

"So, what's the decision going to be, gentlemen? Do we go ahead with Trent's offer, which sounds pretty good to me, or try to find another way to resolve this?" Sheriff Rawlins was anxious to finalize the plans for the Babbitt family, Joanne and her two kids, Alma and Tommy. The jewelry had been returned, and, as Jerrod had anticipated, everyone understood the circumstances. To a family, they decided to go along with any decision the sheriff made on how to handle the punishment for the thefts, but it was Trent who had offered a solution on how to proceed.

"Sounds reasonable to me, sheriff." Doc Minton had thought Trent's plan made perfect sense.

"I agree with Doc," Sam said. "It works out for everyone."

"You'll get no argument from me," Niall smiled. He still couldn't believe his good fortune. Kate would be his in a little over a week. "He picks up a housekeeper and cook, now that he's losing the one he has," Niall nodded at Trent, "plus gets one experienced ranch hand, and one that appears to be a quick learner. And we've the knowledge they'll be watched over by an ex-lawman, even if he can be a little hot headed."

The last brought a smile from Trent. The week had been a blur, but things were working out for his daughter and the fifteen-year-old-boy he'd met so many years ago. He would never have foreseen it, but watching Kate and Niall together these past few days was all the confirmation he needed to believe they'd build a solid life together.

"Then it's settled. Trent, the Babbitt's are officially remanded into your custody for a period of one year. After that, if all goes well, they'll be free to go about their business, or perhaps even stay on with you at the ranch," the sheriff said, then added, "as long as you're sure you want to go through with this."

"No doubts, Sheriff. Mrs. Babbitt is grateful for the work and housing, and Tommy is as excited as you'd expect to start learning to ranch. Alma's a bit of a hard case, but then who wouldn't be, with what she's gone through. My gut tells me the girl has a good heart. What kid steals jewelry just to give it to her Ma to make her happy? They never intended to sell any of it. Only wanted to raise their Ma's spirits, help her get well."

Trent shook his head, still not quite believing the reason Alma had taken the small amounts of jewelry. But it all made sense now that the whole story was out. She'd be a handful, but between him and Josh, Trent thought they could help Alma sort things out, allow her to finish growing up without the burden of supporting her Ma and brother.

"You know, Trent, there are some ladies in town who don't think it's proper, you having an unmarried woman out at the ranch." Sam saw the disgusted look on Trent's face but continued. "Just saying, there are some who may doubt your motives. Now that Mrs. Babbitt's well, it's apparent she's a fine-looking woman, and smart. She has lousy taste in men, judging by the actions of her husband, but she's a good woman, nonetheless. Watch yourself, my friend." Sam slapped Trent on the back and laughed at the incredulous look on the ex-lawman's face.

Epilogue

Saturday arrived with clear skies to welcome the guests who'd been invited to witness the ceremony. Even with such short notice, everyone came to the MacLaren ranch to celebrate the union. Whereas no one had thought Niall should marry Jocelyn, everyone felt the opposite about Kate. She was well liked and loved by more than just Niall.

Beth couldn't contain herself. She was getting a new mama, and it was the best person ever. She danced around, talking non-stop, then wandered off to play with the other children. Every time Kate looked at Beth, her new daughter, she felt her heart swell, and she knew for certain she'd made the right decision.

Drew and Will had expressed how glad they were that Kate would be a permanent part of their family. Will and Emily were now engaged and Kate looked forward to having a sister-in-law in the not-too-distant future. The twins had offered to stay in the bunkhouse a few nights to give Niall and Kate some privacy since a honeymoon would have to wait. With Alicia and Beth staying with the Jacobsons for a few nights, Kate smiled at the thought of her and her husband's first night alone.

It was a gift indeed that Jamie was able to stay for the wedding. He mingled with everyone, laughed, drank, and seemed to be having a fabulous time. His initial anger at his brother had been replaced with a warm acceptance of Kate and the knowledge that she'd make his brother happy.

Looking at his brother, Niall knew the wedding had been hard for him to witness. Niall remembered the depth of Jamie's love for the woman who'd betrayed him. Victoria, the woman who was to have been his wife. Jamie had never loved another, never come close, but he'd built a life for himself away from Fire Mountain and the memories. Niall hoped that someday Jamie would return for good and reclaim his stake in the ranch.

"He seems so alone, Alicia," Kate said as they both watched Jamie mingle. As much as he tried, he never appeared to relax, let down his guard.

"Well, no matter what that boy says, he may never get over losing Victoria. That girl broke his heart, taking off the way she did," Alicia replied. After all this time, Victoria leaving still didn't make sense to her. Something had never seemed right. But Jamie had refused to go after her, and wasn't one to forgive.

Strong arms came up behind Kate, wrapped around her waist, and drew her back, up against his firm chest. Kate let out a sigh and turned her head up to see Niall smiling down over her shoulder. "And what are you two ladies talking about?"

"Oh, Jamie. And Victoria," his aunt said. "I still don't understand, Niall. All the things we knew about Victoria, how loyal she was, and how in love she was with Jamie. For her to pick up and leave still makes my stomach churn. It wasn't like the girl, is all I'm saying. I still think something happened to make her leave."

"You know, there are always two sides to any story. Sounds like no one has ever heard Victoria's,"

Kate said. She wished she'd known both people when they were young. "Maybe someday she'll get the chance to tell it."

"Could be you're right, Kate. But Jamie refused to consider it then, and refuses to think about her now. He's a good man, but unforgiving." Niall still remembered their fights on this issue, but didn't want to dwell on it today, his wedding day.

"Are you happy?" Niall whispered in Kate's ear.

"Yes. You?"

"Very. But I'll be happier when everyone leaves and we have the house to ourselves. Do you think anyone would miss us if we snuck back inside now?" Niall resumed placing soft kisses on her neck.

Kate laughed at his question and began to respond, when a shout went up from a rider racing toward the gathering. It was Tom, from the telegraph office, and he was yelling for Hen Wright.

"Hen! I've got an urgent telegram for you. Niall, sorry to barge in like this," Tom apologized.

"No need, Tom. How about a drink?"

"Thanks but I need to give Hen the telegram and head back to town. Marshal," Tom looked at Jamie, "you may want to see this, too."

Hen came up and took the message Tom offered him. He opened it and read, his face turning to stone. He read it again, then turned to find Jamie. He walked to the lawman, halting a couple of feet away.

"Victoria's been kidnapped."

Other books in the MacLarens of Fire Mountain series

by Shirleen Davies

Faster than the Rest

Handsome, ruthless, young, US Marshal Jamie MacLaren had lost everything—his parents, his family connections, and his childhood sweetheart—but he's back and better than ever. Just as he successfully reconnects with his family and starts to rebuild his life, he gets the unexpected and unwanted assignment of rescuing the woman who broke his heart.

Beautiful, wealthy, Victoria Wicklund chose money and power over love, but is now fighting for her life—or is she? Who has she become in the seven years since she left Fire Mountain to take up her life in San Francisco? Is she really as innocent as she says?

Marshal MacLaren struggles to learn the truth and do his job, but the past and present lead him in different directions as his heart and brain wage battle. Is Victoria a victim or a villain? Is life offering him another chance, or just another heart-break?

In this fast paced Western Romance, Jamie and Victoria struggle against all odds to uncover past secrets and come to grips with a passion that knows no reason.

About the Author

Shirleen Davies began her new series, MacLarens of Fire Mountain with Tougher than the Rest, the story of the oldest brother, Niall MacLaren. During the day she provides consulting services to small and mid-sized businesses. But her real passion is writing emotionally charged stories of flawed people who find redemption through love and acceptance. She grew up in Southern California and now lives with her husband in a beautiful town in northern Arizona. Between them they are the proud parents of five grown sons.

Shirleen loves to hear from her readers.
Write to her at shirleen@shirleendavies.com
Visit her at www.shirleendavies.com
Thank you!

Made in the USA
Coppell, TX
27 July 2021

59571759R10125